"You never did say what you were doing out here this late at night,"

Jonah said.

"I couldn't sleep," Kat lied. "What are you doing here?"

"I couldn't sleep either." He kept looking at her with that same I-can-lie-as-well-as-you-can expression on his handsome face.

She turned, planning to take off, but he moved too fast.

One hand came to rest at the small of her back as his lips unerringly found hers.

She would have fought both him and the kiss, but he had taken her by surprise and left her reeling when it ended abruptly.

"I hate having regrets," he said matter-of-factly, then turned and left her on the deserted dock without another word, leaving her to stare after him, the taste and feel of him still on her lips.

It seemed he had no qualms about leaving her with one *big* regret—that she wouldn't be kissing him again.

Dear Harlequin Intrigue Reader,

Harlequin Intrigue has four new stories to blast you out of the winter doldrums. Look what we've got heating up for you this month.

Sylvie Kurtz brings you the first in her two-book miniseries FLESH AND BLOOD. Fifteen years ago, a burst of anger by the banks of the raging Red Thunder River changed the lives of two brothers forever. In *Remembering Red Thunder*, Sheriff Chance Conover struggles to regain the memory of his life, his wife and their unborn baby before a man out for revenge silences him permanently.

You can also look for the second book in the four-book continuity series MORIAH'S LANDING— *Howling in the Darkness* by B.J. Daniels. Jonah Ries has always sensed something was wrong in Moriah's Landing, but when he accidentally crashes Kat Ridgemont's online blind date, he realizes the tough yet fragile beauty has more to fear than even the town's superstitions.

In *Operation: Reunited* by Linda O. Johnston, Alexa Kenner is on the verge of marriage when she meets John O'Rourke, a man who eerily resembles her dead lover, Cole Rappaport, who died in a terrible explosion. Could they be one and the same?

And finally this month, one by one government witnesses who put away a mob associate have been killed, with only Tara Ford remaining. U.S. Deputy Marshal Brad Harrison vows to protect Tara by placing her *In His Safekeeping*— by Shawna Delacorte.

We hope you enjoy these books, and remember to come back next month for more selections from MORIAH'S LANDING and FLESH AND BLOOD!

Sincerely,

Denise O'Sullivan
Associate Senior Editor
Harlequin Intrigue

HOWLING IN THE DARKNESS
B.J. DANIELS

HARLEQUIN®

TORONTO • NEW YORK • LONDON
AMSTERDAM • PARIS • SYDNEY • HAMBURG
STOCKHOLM • ATHENS • TOKYO • MILAN • MADRID
PRAGUE • WARSAW • BUDAPEST • AUCKLAND

Special thanks and acknowledgment
are given to B.J. Daniels for her contribution
to the MORIAH'S LANDING series.

ISBN 0-373-22654-3

HOWLING IN THE DARKNESS

ABOUT THE AUTHOR

A former award-winning journalist, B.J. Daniels is the author of thirty-seven short stories and fourteen novels. Most of her books are set in Montana, where she lives with her husband, Parker; two springer spaniels, Zoey and Scout; and a temperamental tomcat named Jeff. Her first novel, *Odd Man Out,* was nominated for the *Romantic Times* Reviewer's Choice Award for best first book and best Harlequin Intrigue. B.J. is a member of Bozeman Writers Group and Romance Writers of America. When not writing, she enjoys reading, camping and fishing, and snowboarding. Write to her at: P.O. Box 183, Bozeman MT 59771.

Books by B.J. Daniels

HARLEQUIN INTRIGUE
312—ODD MAN OUT
353—OUTLAWED!
417—HOTSHOT P.I.
446—UNDERCOVER CHRISTMAS
493—A FATHER FOR HER BABY
533—STOLEN MOMENTS
555—LOVE AT FIRST SIGHT
566—INTIMATE SECRETS
585—THE AGENT'S SECRET CHILD
604—MYSTERY BRIDE
617—SECRET BODYGUARD
643—A WOMAN WITH A MYSTERY
654—HOWLING IN THE DARKNESS

Don't miss any of our special offers. Write to us at the following address for information on our newest releases.

Harlequin Reader Service
U.S.: 3010 Walden Ave., P.O. Box 1325, Buffalo, NY 14269
Canadian: P.O. Box 609, Fort Erie, Ont. L2A 5X3

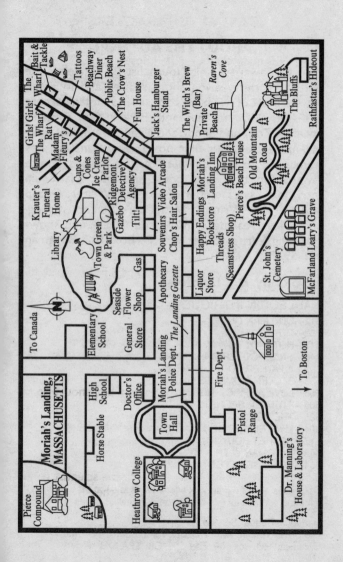

CAST OF CHARACTERS

Jonah Ries—The FBI agent has more to fear in Moriah's Landing than even he knows.

Kat Ridgemont—The private investigator has a deadly secret admirer after her.

Arabella Leigh—Is she as crazy as everyone thinks she is when she warns Kat of danger and death?

McFarland Leary—His ghost is due to rise again.

Cassandra Quintana—What does the fortune-teller see in the cards that she isn't telling?

Ernie McDougal—Is the shy Bait & Tackle shop owner into more than fish and lures?

Emily Ridgemont—The seventeen-year-old has a secret of her own.

Brody Ries—The owner of the Wharf Rat bar will do anything for money.

Tommy Cavendish—The fifteen-year-old doesn't know what he is getting into.

Deke Turner—The former FBI agent comes to Moriah's Landing with only one thing on his mind: revenge.

Marley Glasgow—He hates women. But enough to kill?

Max Weathers—The FBI agent disappeared after being sent to Moriah's Landing to investigate an anonymous tip.

Dr. Leland Manning—How far will the scientist go in his quest to discover the secret in witches' descendants' genes?

Leslie Ridgemont—She might be dead, but in Moriah's Landing that doesn't mean she is gone for good.

This one is for Jeff Robinson, a great writer, a great friend. Not only has he always supported my career—but he keeps my husband, Parker, busy playing basketball so I can write. Thanks, Jeff!

Chapter One

A killer fog rolled in off the Atlantic, moving silently through the darkness as it approached the small town nestled at the edge of the sea.

Jonah Ries didn't see the fog coming any more than he could see the future. But he felt it. At first just a disquieting sense of foreboding. Then he came roaring up over a rise in the rocky landscape and saw the sign, Welcome to Moriah's Landing, and he knew, a soul-deep knowing, that this was the last place on earth he should be.

He slowed his motorcycle, the feeling of darkness so strong he could see himself flipping a U-turn in the middle of the road, throttling up the bike, his taillight growing dimmer and dimmer beneath the twisted dark limbs snaking over the pavement.

But he could no more turn back than he could convince himself he had nothing to fear in Moriah's Landing. He knew what he would risk coming here. A hell of a lot more than just his life, he thought as he swept down the hill, passing St. John's Cemetery without looking in that direction, and heading for the wharf.

Overhead, a half-moon rode the star-specked sky, reminding him he had five days, tops.

He felt the first hint of the fog long before he saw it. Small patches of dampness brushed past his face, ghostlike as spiderwebs. But the moment he turned down Waterfront Avenue, the mist moved in as thick as wet concrete, obliterating everything, forcing him to pull over, park his bike and walk the rest of the way.

Might as well just get it over with. He reached under the left side of his leather jacket for the reassuring feel of his .38 nestled in the shoulder holster. Snug as a bug. Too bad what he feared most couldn't be killed with a bullet. Not even a silver one.

He made his way along the brick sidewalk toward the faint beat of the neon bar sign at the end of the street, unable to throw off the ominous feeling he'd gotten at just the sight of the town's sign.

Nor had he realized how late it was until he noticed that the shops were all dark, locked up for the night. Of course, it wasn't Memorial Day yet. That's when the tiny Massachusetts town would come alive with tourists, especially this year, with Moriah's Landing celebrating its 350th anniversary.

Tourists would flock here for the beach—and the witch folklore, bringing a morbid fascination for the town's dark, witch-hanging past.

Tonight, though, the small township lay cloaked in a fog of obscurity, silent as McFarland Leary's grave, as if waiting for something to happen. Unfortunately, Jonah feared he knew what that something was.

"Hey!" A voice came out of the darkness from the end of the street near the blurred, flashing bar sign for the Wharf Rat. Jonah could barely make out the form, but instantly recognized it, just as the man coming out of the bar had recognized him.

"Hey." The man staggered forward, then stopped, clearly jarred momentarily from his drunken state.

Jonah reached blindly for the first door next to him, grabbed the handle and turned, praying it wouldn't be locked, but prepared to use whatever it took to get in. He shoved with his shoulder as he turned the handle, losing his balance in surprise as the door fell open and he stumbled in, closing it behind him.

"You're late," a female voice admonished.

He froze, his back to the dark room. From beyond it, a narrow path of light ran across the carpet to his feet. He turned slowly, comforted by the feel of the .38.

She stood behind a large antique desk, one hand on her hip, her head cocked to the side so her long mane of raven's-wing-black hair hung down past her shoulder like a wave. He could feel her gaze, dark and searching, long before he stepped close enough to really see her face.

"Sorry," he said without thinking. He had plenty to be sorry about so he didn't mind.

Her eyes narrowed. "I guess you didn't get my last e-mail."

He shook his head. Unfortunately, he hadn't gotten any of her e-mails.

"Are you ready?" she asked, sounding a little unsure of herself. He sensed this was new territory for her.

Ready? He watched her pick up her purse and jacket

and then hesitate. He couldn't help but stare at her. She had the most interesting face he'd ever seen. Wide-set dark navy-blue eyes with dense lashes, a full, almost pouty, mouth and high cheekbones, all put together in a way that startled and interested him at the same time.

"Yes?" she asked, eyeing him, definitely not sure now. "Is there a problem?"

Not unless being totally confused was a problem. He started to tell her that she was making a mistake. But then she came around the corner of the desk and he got the full effect of her little black dress.

Wow. It was a knockout on her, formfitting against the warm olive glow of her skin. Silver glittered on her wrist, dangled from the lobes of her ears and swept the curve of her neck and throat. Nestled in the hollow between her breasts hung a small silver lighthouse charm.

"Did you have some spot in mind?" she asked. The tap of her heels drew his attention back up to her face as she moved toward him.

He had lots of spots in mind. But she'd caught him on a night when he was already off-kilter and she was the last thing he'd expected to run across. So it took him longer than it should have to realize she thought he was her date—an online blind date, it seemed. Even worse. And from the way she was dressed, they were going out for a drink. Maybe a late supper.

Unfortunately, her "real" date would probably be along any minute. Jonah realized he'd be damn disappointed when that happened. The problem was, leaving here right now wasn't an option.

At least not out the *front* door where he feared the man he'd seen would be looking for him.

Past her, he saw a way out—literally. A back exit and a chance to kill two birds with one stone, so to speak.

"How about the Moriah's Landing Inn?" he asked, realizing he had a better chance with her than alone if he hoped to avoid the man he'd just seen in the street. The hotel was only a few doors up on Main Street and had a very nice restaurant. And it was easy to get to since he figured he was probably supposed to be driving a car. Which he wasn't. More important, they could get to it quickly by going down the narrow alley out back, therefore cutting down the chance of an ugly confrontation with his past.

"Great," she said, sounding a little surprised.

Probably because of the way he looked. "I apologize for the way I'm dressed," he said, glancing down at the jeans, biking boots and the laundry-worn blue chambray shirt he wore underneath his old brown leather jacket. He ran a hand over his stubbled jaw, then raked it on up through his hair. Not exactly hot-date material.

She looked down at her dress. It hit about thigh-high on her legs. Black platform sandals gave her a few more inches in height, putting them on about the same level. Her eyes came back to him, a tantalizing flush to her cheeks. "Is the dress too—"

"It's perfect," he said, meaning it. "You look sensational." Meaning that, too.

She quirked a smile at him and ducked her head. "Thanks."

Yes, definitely new territory for her. This was a woman who didn't often feel vulnerable. But she did right now. He couldn't help but wonder why. Even if he hadn't had to make a quick getaway, her vulnerability made him all the more anxious to get her out of here before her real date arrived.

He glanced out the front window toward the street, the fog dense as chowder. No sign of the dark figure he'd seen earlier. "Why don't we go out the back? It's closer that way."

She lifted an eyebrow but said nothing. He helped her with her jacket, wondering how much she knew about her real date, and opened the back door, glancing down the quaint brick alley to make sure no one was waiting for him.

As they left, he noticed the small sign hanging over the back door. Ridgemont Detective Agency. She worked for a private investigator? Just his luck.

He could hear music and the faint murmur of voices traveling on the sea breeze coming up from Raven's Cove. His heart picked up the beat of her heels tapping the brick as they walked closer to the wharf, wrapped in the dense cloak of the fog, making what was already an unimaginable night surreal.

He told himself he'd just stolen someone else's date. That alone could explain his uneasiness. Also he was home again, back in a town he'd vowed never to return to. Unfortunately, he knew only too well all the things that could be lurking in Moriah's Landing.

She took his arm, the dark alley almost intimate as the foghorn groaned out past the cove. He breathed in her scent and tried to relax. He was safe with her. But he knew relaxing would be impossible as long as he was in Moriah's Landing. And dangerous.

The apparition came out of the mist so unexpectedly Jonah didn't even have time to reach for his weapon, let alone sense the presence. Suddenly a dark figure appeared in front of them, her black hooded cloak blowing out in the breeze like the wings of a vulture.

He started at the sight of the old crone, her gray hair a silver aura sticking out from under her black hood, her eyes bottomless holes in her wrinkled face.

Reflexively he stepped between his date and the old woman as the crone reached clawlike gnarled fingers toward them.

"It's just Arabella," his date whispered. "She's harmless."

How little she knew.

The old woman's gaze locked with his for an instant, then she stumbled back as if she'd seen a ghost. Or something worse. "Katherine," she cried, fear contorting her face as she gasped for breath and reached around him, trying to pluck at the fabric of his date's jacket sleeve.

"Danger comes in with the fog," the crone croaked, her gaze on Jonah. "Danger and *death*." Then the old woman stumbled back into the mist, leaving Jonah shaken. If he couldn't even sense an old woman coming in the fog, how did he plan to protect himself from the real trouble here?

Katherine must have seen his expression. "Arabella's just local color," she said with a laugh, and pulled him toward the Moriah's Landing Inn. "I wouldn't be surprised if the town council paid her to freak out visitors as part of our witch-folklore ambience.''

Jonah looked over his shoulder. The old woman was gone. But like him, she'd sensed something had come in with the fog, unleashing evil in Moriah's Landing.

They walked past one of the ''witch'' shops along the narrow alley that peddled magic, from herbs and oils to tarot cards and crystals.

''I'm sure you've heard about all this foolishness?'' his date asked as she glanced into the shop window, then at him.

''What foolishness?'' he asked, pretending he didn't know and that he wasn't still shaken by their run-in with Arabella.

''Witches, the supernatural, all the hype that comes with Moriah's Landing,'' she said with a laugh. ''According to local legend, early resident McFarland Leary was a consort to a witch.''

They crossed Main Street to the entrance of the Moriah's Landing Inn. He opened the door for her, anxious to get inside. Because of the hour, the hotel lobby and the restaurant were nearly empty. A young waiter showed them to a table by the window facing the cove—farthest away from the door and Main Street.

''When they started burning witches at the stake in Salem, many of the witches fled to Moriah's Landing where they were hidden by McFarland Leary and his consort, a witch named Seama,'' she said, and nervously plucked up her cloth napkin from the table. ''Seama and her secret coven give the town its supernatural ambience.''

She glanced at him, then out at the foggy darkness

as if there was nothing to fear beyond the window. "McFarland Leary is our resident ghost, cursed by the witch he betrayed." She swung her gaze back to him. Definitely nervous, making him pretty sure she didn't know much about him. "Seama was carrying Leary's child when she caught him cheating on her with a mortal and she damned him for eternity. Then she disappeared with her unborn baby. Some people swear she later returned to town and her descendants live among us." She smiled at that. "The town accused Leary of being a warlock and sentenced him to die. Warlocks were used for kindling around the stakes to get the fire going hot enough to burn the witches. But Moriah's Landing likes to be different. The town hung Leary from a big oak tree on the town green and buried him in St. John's Cemetery as a warning to others who might want to consort with witches. Now Leary rises from his grave every five years to seek revenge on the town. Or at least that's what the chamber of commerce wants you to believe."

She took a breath as she finished her story and let out a little tense laugh. "Welcome to Moriah's Landing."

Obviously, her real date wasn't from town. He smiled, gazing intently into her dark blue eyes, anxious to change the subject, no matter what it took, even if it meant flirting with a beautiful woman. "I like it already, Katherine." At least Arabella had provided him with his date's name.

"Kat." She dropped her gaze, a faint blush rising in her cheeks, making her even more appealing, as if she wasn't already. "Everyone just calls me Kat."

Except for Arabella. He glanced toward Waterfront Avenue, the fog too thick to know if the man he'd seen was still out there looking for him. "You sound as if you don't like the town," he said, not sure how much he was supposed to know about her but determined to keep her talking about herself so she didn't start questioning him. "What makes you stay?"

She seemed surprised and he feared he'd already messed up. He wasn't ready to go back out on the street. Even if it had been safe, he found his "date" intriguing. Maybe too intriguing.

She took a sip from her water glass, then picked up her menu. "I've never even thought about leaving. Can you believe it? I didn't even leave to go away to college."

So she went to the all-girl Heathrow College at the edge of town.

"I'm eighth generation," she said as if that explained it. "In Massachusetts you aren't considered a native unless you have at least eight generations buried in the local cemetery."

A local girl. Just his luck.

"Your ancestors must have been fishermen," he guessed, opening his own menu, although he wasn't in the least bit hungry.

"Seventh generation," she said. "Dad died at sea when I was a sophomore in college."

"I'm sorry."

She nodded and peered at him over her menu, her wide blue eyes magnetic. "Commercial fishing," she said, then dropped her gaze again behind the menu.

He nodded to himself, more than aware that the sea

had always taken men from small fishing villages like Moriah's Landing and would continue to as long as men went to sea. And men would always be drawn to the sea. Some forces in nature pulled at you with a witchery that Jonah understood better than most.

"What about your mother?" he asked, hoping his question was general enough.

"My mother—" he heard the catch in her throat, the hesitation in her voice "—died when I was three. I can't remember her." She closed her menu, clearly closing the subject.

"I'm sorry. I hope that isn't all the family you have here," he said, doing a little fishing of his own.

"There's my half sister, Emily. She's seventeen and a real handful, but I love her. She's all the family I have left and she graduates from high school next week. Tell me more about you."

More about him. He studied his menu wondering about the man she was supposed to be having dinner with tonight. He could only guess that they met online, considering her comment about getting her e-mail, and that they obviously hadn't met face-to-face—until to-night. He knew nothing about online dating. But it was pretty clear that she didn't know her date very well—nor he her. "There isn't much to tell."

"Your father wasn't a fisherman, I'll bet."

Far from it. He shook his head and smiled as he lowered his menu. Fortunately, the waiter saved him. "I have to have lobster," Jonah told her. "How about you?"

"I don't eat seafood." She shook her head. "Not because of any moral stand or because of my father.

I've just never liked it. I'll take the chicken,'' she said to the waiter.

"Kat,'' Jonah said, trying out the name. He liked it. It fit her. "You must know practically everyone in town.'' Cause for concern.

"Everyone,'' she said, and laughed.

She would know his family. The thought left him cold.

"It's one of the problems of living in a small town,'' she said. "Everyone knows everything about you. And you them.'' She shrugged. "But it's home, you know?''

He didn't know. He glanced out the window toward the wharf. The neon from the bars at the end of Waterfront gave the fog an eerie glow.

"You can't even see the lighthouse tonight the fog is so thick,'' Kat said, following his gaze to the night, sounding worried about fishermen who might be trying to get to safe harbor.

Jonah looked out past Raven's Cove, where he knew the lighthouse loomed up from a jagged island outcropping of rock, then back at her as the waiter brought their salads. He couldn't stop thinking about Arabella's warning. Or his own uneasiness. He told himself it was just the fog. Just being back here.

"So tell me about your work,'' Kat said.

He watched her take a bite of her salad, captivated by her mouth. "My work?''

"Computers. What is it exactly that you do?''

He let out a laugh. So he was supposed to be a computer nerd? Great. "It's too boring for words. I'm sure your job is much more interesting.''

She shook her head, smiling. "You aren't one of those people who thinks the private-eye business is like on TV?" She had a great smile. He felt heat as his gaze locked with hers.

"You mean it's not?" he asked, trying to sound disappointed as he looked deep into all that blue. It was like looking down into the sea. Bottomless and full of mysteries.

She licked her lips, her cheeks flushing again, and dropped her gaze to her salad, her fork poised above a piece of endive. "It actually consists of tedious, time-consuming hours spent digging up facts. But I started the business because I wanted to help people, so I don't mind." She shrugged and let her gaze lift to his again.

He didn't know if the jolt he felt came from her look—or the realization that she *was* the P.I. of Ridge-mont Detective Agency. Bad news. But although he was more than a little attracted to her, he wouldn't be seeing her again after tonight. In fact, he planned to be out of Moriah's Landing as quickly as possible. As soon as he finished what he'd come here to do.

He managed to steer the conversation away from himself throughout the rest of their dinner date, careful not to give anything away—or let on that he wasn't her real date. He even got her to relax a little.

"I had a nice time," she said shyly outside the restaurant after dinner, sounding surprised. Why did he get the feeling that she didn't date much?

"I had a nice time, too," he said, realizing it was true. He hadn't meant for the date to last this long. He could no longer pretend he was just buying time. And yet he felt off balance again out here in the fog, being with this woman who should have been with someone else. "Can I walk you home?"

She shook her head. "I just live a block or so from here." She tugged her jacket around her and shifted her feet. Her gaze came up to meet his. Oh, those eyes. And that mouth.

Stirred by a yearning stronger than the force of the moon on the sea, he bent to kiss her good-night. Good-bye.

Her eyes fluttered closed. Her lips parted. A hair-breadth from her wonderful mouth Jonah felt something brush the back of his neck, something cold as the kiss of death.

He jerked around, only to see wisps of fog streaming past as if blown up from the sea by a gust of wind. Except there was no wind, just as there was no one right behind him. But that didn't mean there wasn't a presence out there in the mist watching them. "Let me walk you home."

She opened her eyes in surprise, licked her lips and turned her face away, unsure. Again. "I am more than capable of walking myself home." Obviously upset with him for not kissing her, she took a couple of steps backward.

"I had a great time," he said, not wanting to let her go. Suddenly afraid to let her go.

She nodded, turned and disappeared into the fog.

He waited and then followed her at a distance as she walked to her clapboard three-story house at the edge of the town green, unable to shake the feeling he'd had that instant before he'd almost kissed her.

Before turning back to the wharf, he listened for the sound of the bolt sliding on her door, and then for the footsteps he'd heard to retreat, shaken by the fact that someone else had followed her home as well.

Chapter Two

Kat couldn't lose the odd feeling that had come over her outside the restaurant. It wasn't just that her date hadn't kissed her. Or that he seemed to cool toward her. As she'd walked home, she'd heard footsteps behind her on the brick pathway. Two sets.

When she'd stop, so did the others, which only strengthened an illogical but growing fear that someone was after her—just as someone had been after her mother twenty years before. The Beretta in her purse and the fact that she was an expert markswoman, had given her little comfort tonight. She'd been spooked and running scared, both highly unlike her.

Once inside her house, she closed the door behind her, locked it, then pulled aside the curtain to look out into the fog, seeing nothing, hearing nothing but her own ragged breath and the erratic thump of her heart. Logically, she knew the sound of the footsteps had probably been some weird echo because of the fog, just as she knew what had caused this sudden case of paranoia. The very mention of her mother.

She kicked off her heels and padded barefoot farther into the first floor of the house she'd lived in her whole life, noticing as she looked upstairs that a light shone from under her sister Emily's bedroom door. She could hear music playing and Em on the phone talking with one of her friends, both reassuring sounds. She was glad the seventeen-year-old was home on a school night and would be graduating next week, although it worried her that her half sister didn't seem to have any plans after graduation. But tonight, Kat was just glad not to be alone in the house.

As she passed the phone on the small table at the bottom of the stairs, she noticed that the answering-machine light was flashing. Distractedly, she hit Rewind. She still felt a little scared and wished she'd taken her date up on his offer to escort her. But wasn't that possibly the mistake her mother had made? Trusting a man? The wrong man.

She hugged herself as the answering-machine tape stopped. What was wrong with her? Her date had been perfectly nice. He'd made her laugh. He'd made her forget how uncomfortable she'd felt about online blind dating. He'd seemed interested in her, in her work. And she couldn't discount the obvious attraction she'd felt for him.

But once they were outside the restaurant, he'd started to kiss her and hadn't—as much as she'd wanted him to. Why was that? Not out of shyness, that was for sure.

And yet he'd seemed almost scared of her at first. The way he'd come into her office, appearing confused. Late. Showing up looking as if he'd just gotten off work at the docks. She'd been nervous about meeting him. But he'd seemed nervous, too.

And he hadn't been the nervous type. Nor had he been anything like she'd expected. The strong jawline, dark from a day's stubble, the deep brown eyes, a shade lighter than his short brown hair. He'd looked more muscular, rugged..dangerous than she'd expected.

The thought startled her. She'd already been the dangerous-man route. Just the once. But a smart woman learned the first time. Or she ended up dead on the town green. She didn't want to be the kind of woman who picked the wrong man. Like her mother.

Kat shoved that thought away and hit the play button on the answering machine.

"Hi, it's Ross."

Her head jerked up, her attention dragged from her date—to the voice on the answering machine.

"Sorry about tonight. I really wanted to meet you in person, but something came up at the last minute. Maybe we could do it another time? See you online."

Disbelieving, she pushed rewind and listened to the message again. Her online date had stood her up?

She felt a chill. Then who had she just spent dinner with?

Desperately, she tried to remember what the man had told her about himself during their meal. Only vague generalities that could have fit any man! No wonder he'd seemed surprised when he'd come into her office. No wonder he'd seemed so interested in her, in her work. Because he knew nothing about her! And he didn't want her asking too many questions about him. She'd been so nervous, she hadn't even noticed. Until now.

A thought struck her. Maybe his interest in her hadn't been just to cover his deception. Scared, she tried to remember what she'd told him about herself. Why had he pretended to be her date?

She felt sick inside. Normally, she was damn good at reading people. But dating—God, it made her so anxious. Probably because it had been so long and she'd been so scared that he would turn out to be another Mr. Wrong. Mr. Dead Wrong. And maybe he had been. Thank God she hadn't let him walk her home. She hugged herself, suddenly cold. Had his been one of the set of footsteps she'd heard following her home? The thought froze her to her core.

"Sorry about your date."

Kat looked up the stairs as Emily leaned over the railing in her favorite, worn-thin teddy-bear pajamas. Emily was small and slim with their father's gray eyes. She'd pulled her dark, shoulder length hair into a ponytail, making her look even younger than her seventeen years. "I saved the message for you. What a jerk. He didn't even come up with a decent excuse for standing you up." She frowned. "Have you been working all this time?"

She considered lying. "No, I…went out to dinner."

"By *yourself?*" Emily made it sound as if she couldn't imagine anything worse. She probably couldn't.

"No, actually, I met someone." She tried to assure herself that it had been innocent, needing desperately to believe that. He'd just taken advantage of the situation. What man wouldn't who saw the chance to have dinner with a young woman in a sexy black dress? *An honest man. A man with nothing to hide.*

"Who *was* this guy?" Emily asked, coming down the stairs to eye her more closely.

Kat wished she'd lied and said she'd worked late. "No one you know," she said defensively, unable to forget that she'd been attracted to him, a man who lied to her. "I don't need to have my dates checked out by you." She flipped off the downstairs light, picked up her black platform heels where she'd dropped them by the door and started up the steps past her sister, hoping that was the end of it.

"As if you don't give *me* the third degree about every guy I date," Emily said, trailing after her.

"That's different," Kat said, stopping on the landing. "I'm twenty-three. You're seventeen and you still have a lot to learn about men."

Emily rolled her eyes. "As if *you're* the authority on men. I've dated more this year than you have in your life!" She swept into her room, slamming the door behind her. Emily always had to get in the last word.

Kat stared after her, just wishing the last word hadn't been the truth. Tonight proved how little Kat knew about men. In spades.

She climbed to her own bedroom on the third floor, not bothering to turn on a light. The room was large with two bay windows on each side and a tiny, railed widow's walk at the end facing the town green and, past it, Raven's Cove and the Atlantic. Light filtered in from the pale gray fog.

She dropped her shoes beside the bed and, opening

the French doors, stepped out onto the walk into the damp mist, feeling oddly vulnerable. She no longer felt safe—not when she couldn't trust her judgment any more than she had tonight. Who *had* she gone to dinner with?

She drew in a breath of the cool, wet night air and looked out at the wisps of mist moving like ghosts through the town green, trying to convince herself that she wasn't her mother. But more and more when she looked in the mirror, she saw the startling resemblance to the old photographs of her mother.

Worse, she feared the similarities were more than skin deep, since her first choice of a man had been deadly wrong, a choice she'd paid for dearly a year ago. Now, it seemed, she'd made another mistake tonight, and to think she'd been tempted to let him walk her home.

The fog drifted across the green, weaving in and out of the trees. She caught a glimpse of the gazebo just beyond the wide sweeping branches of the witch-hanging tree, the white lattice of the gazebo dark with its cloak of dense ivy. It had been on a night like this almost twenty years ago—she shuddered and stepped back inside to close and lock the doors. How could she not help but think of her mother tonight?

KAT WOKE IN A SWEAT, the sheets tangled around her, her heart pounding. She sat up, terrified. Her hand shook as she reached to fumble on the lamp beside her bed, frantically trying to fight off the horrible images that surfaced to consciousness within her. The clock beside her bed read 2:28 a.m.

She'd had the dream again. Only this time, she swore she could smell her mother's perfume. And for a moment, she would have sworn she wasn't alone in the room.

She hugged herself as she glanced around her bedroom, seeing nothing but familiar objects—and no place for anyone to hide. After a few minutes, she curled back under the covers and, although she fought sleep and the possibility of the nightmare coming back, she finally dozed off again.

She woke to the sound of the radio alarm. It jolted her out of bed, dragging remnants of the nightmare with her. She stumbled to the bathroom, disrobing to step into the shower. The hot water and the light of day helped. By the time she dried off, she'd convinced herself that there'd been nothing to fear last night— including the dream and her mystery date.

Logically, if he'd meant her harm, he wouldn't have taken her to the Moriah's Landing Inn on Main Street. He'd have suggested someplace where there was less chance of them being seen together. And even though she'd heard footsteps on her way home, it didn't mean whoever it was had been following her.

By the time she'd dressed for work, she'd discounted her fears from the previous night, even coming up with a logical explanation for the nightmare's return after all these years. The twentieth anniversary of her mother's death was only days away. Just the mention of her mother and her death had no doubt spooked her last night on the walk home and triggered the nightmare, even making her believe she smelled her mother's perfume. Just as she'd imagined hearing someone in the room, before her eyes adjusted to the darkness.

But as she left for work, she didn't cut across the town green as she normally did each morning. Her lapse in judgment last night and the dream still had her feeling a little vulnerable. She knew it was crazy, since she was trained to be able to take care of herself in most situations. And what did she have to fear in Moriah's Landing in broad daylight, anyway?

On Main Street she spotted Arabella coming toward her and braced herself for another of the woman's dire warnings of impending doom. But to her surprise, Arabella appeared to cross the street as if to avoid her. Kat saw the poor woman make the sign of the cross and duck down one of the narrow brick alleys.

Normally, Kat found Arabella's bizarre behavior amusing, but this morning it made her a little uneasy.

Worse, Kat found herself looking for her mystery date in the faces she passed. She couldn't help wondering who he was and if she really might have been in danger last night.

As she neared her office, she spotted something lying on the front step. She slowed, glancing around, suddenly feeling as if someone was watching her, waiting for her to find what he'd left for her.

On her office doorstep lay a small bouquet of daisies tied loosely with a short piece of frayed red satin ribbon. No white floral box. No card. Just freshly picked daisies and a worn red ribbon.

As she stooped to lift the flowers gently, as if they were an armed bomb set to blow at even the slightest movement, she told herself they were just flowers.

Nothing sinister about daisies. Of course, they had to be from Ross. A small gesture after standing her up last night. Maybe she'd give him a second chance.

And yet she held the flowers away from her as she opened her office door and, after putting them in a glass vase with water, she set them in the front window away from her desk, away from her sight, anxious to e-mail Ross a thank-you, anxious to find out for sure if he'd left them for her. Or if it had been someone else. Her mystery date?

She checked her messages, not surprised to find one from the insurance company asking her to sign off on Bud Lawson's recent vandalism at his curio shop. Bud was anxious to have it settled so he could get reimbursed for repairs before the start of tourist season—which was only days away.

Since she'd started Ridgemont Detective Agency two·years ago, insurance investigations and workmen's comp made up the bulk of her work, with a few skip traces and domestic-problem cases thrown in. But she loved the work, the slow, methodical plodding that led to a logical conclusion.

She called Bud and set up an appointment for after lunch, then went through the rest of her messages. Her friend Elizabeth had called to remind Kat about her fitting this afternoon at Threads for her dress. She was to be Elizabeth's maid of honor at her upcoming wedding.

Kat couldn't be more happy about Elizabeth's wedding. Dr. Elizabeth Douglas, a criminology professor at the local college, was about to marry a man she'd secretly had a crush on since high school: Cullen Ryan, a detective with the Moriah's Landing Police Department. Kat glanced toward the window, thinking about Elizabeth and the fun they'd had at college. The daisies caught her eye. She felt a flicker of memory and frowned. What was it? Something about daisies. Something unpleasant.

Shaking her head, she checked her e-mail again. Nothing from Ross yet. Her gaze went to the street, as it had so often done all morning. She watched the pedestrians wander by, mostly early tourists.

She realized she was looking again for only one face in the passersby, and after a few moments of not seeing that face, she opened the Lawson case file and reviewed the list of either stolen or vandalized items Bud had sent her. She thumbed through those, making notes, wondering if there wasn't a pattern to the recent rash of vandalisms and robberies in town.

"Hi," a woman's voice said, making Kat jump.

Kat hadn't even heard anyone come in. She looked up from her desk to find her friend Claire standing over her. "Hi, sweetie." She got up to give Claire a hug. "You look great." A lie. Claire looked pale and thin. All those years in the hospital. Just the sight of her made Kat hurt.

But her friend was smiling and she had put on a few much needed pounds.

"I hope I'm not bothering you," Claire said, appearing more anxious than usual and yet obviously trying to hide it. Claire, with her long straight blond hair and large blue eyes, had been so beautiful and carefree before their freshman year at Heathrow College, before one tragic night changed her life forever.

While still beautiful, there was something about Claire now that seemed too brittle, too fragile, as if anything could make her break into a million pieces.

"I thought maybe we could have an early lunch." Claire flashed her a smile, but it seemed a little too bright, as if her friend was trying too hard. "There is something I needed to talk to you about."

Kat glanced at the clock, surprised it was almost eleven-thirty. "That's a great idea." She closed the Lawson file and picked up her purse, curious and yet concerned what that something Claire wanted to discuss might be. "I'm starved."

"Do you mind going to the diner since it's close?" Claire asked.

"Maybe Brie's working and she can join us for a moment if it's not too busy," Kat said.

Claire nodded, but didn't seem enthused about the idea of seeing their friend. Kat wondered what was up. Something.

"Can you believe Elizabeth is getting married in less than two weeks?" Kat said as they started across the street toward the diner. It still surprised her. Of Kat's friends, Elizabeth had always been the serious one, the smart one, the one who'd been more interested in her profession than men compared to the rest of them. She and Elizabeth had drifted apart after college. Only recently had they gotten close again. Kat hadn't realized how much she'd missed her friend and envied Elizabeth finding a man like Cullen. "Who would have thought Elizabeth would ever marry a cop though?"

Kat stopped, realizing that Claire was no longer walking beside her. She turned to see that the woman at Madam Fleury's fortune-telling booth had motioned Claire over.

Kat had seen the dark-haired seer a few times around town and heard through the grapevine that her name was Cassandra Quintana, a fortune-teller hired for the season. While Yvette Castor owned the fortune-telling booth along Waterfront Avenue, it appeared Cassandra had been hired for the upcoming tourist season. No one seemed to know much about the woman—not even Yvette. Protectively, Kat worked her way through the traffic and tourists, unable to imagine what the fortune-teller would want with Claire—except to take advantage of her.

"What's going on?" Kat asked as she joined Claire in front of the brightly colored booth.

Cassandra Quintana raised her dark somber eyes, but said nothing. An attractive woman of about fifty, Cassandra's dyed dark red hair was pulled back under a brilliant-colored bandanna. She wore a glaring geometric-design caftan covered in astrological symbols and dozens of thin multicolored cheap bracelets.

Kat glanced at her friend. Claire appeared paler, if that were possible, and was visibly shaking. "What did you say to upset my friend?"

"She didn't say anything," Claire said, obviously lying.

"Please, let's go. Come on, I'm starved." Claire started across the street toward the diner.

But Kat wasn't through with the fortune-teller. "My friend isn't well," she said the moment Claire was out of earshot. "I won't have you upsetting her with any of your crystal ball crap."

The woman arched an eyebrow, and then with the flick of her wrist—the cluster of cheap tin bracelets jangling—she produced a tarot card as if pulling it from thin air. She dropped the card on the table in front of Kat. It was the devil card. "I charged your friend nothing. You, however, will have to pay me for information about the man you've been looking for all day, but I assure you it will be worth every penny."

Cassandra smiled at her surprise and tapped the card, drawing Kat's attention to the devil's face. Incredibly, it looked a whole lot like her mystery date from last night.

Chapter Three

Kat hurried after Claire, catching her as she stepped inside the diner. "I hope you don't believe any of that mumbo-jumbo stuff. That woman just pulled the devil card out of her sleeve as if that was supposed to scare me." Kat shook her head. "I can't believe those people."

"The *devil* card?" Claire asked, sounding worried as Kat stepped past her to slide into a booth by the window.

"A woman I met at the hospital read tarot cards," Claire said as she took the seat opposite Kat, still looking concerned. "The devil is the fear card. It symbolizes fear of the unknown."

Kat groaned, wishing she hadn't said anything. "It's just the card the woman happened to have up her sleeve, Claire. My only fear is that she said something to upset you."

Claire didn't seem to hear. "The devil card can also be a sign of temptation, the demonic side of you, tempting you in some way."

Kat felt a shadow fall across the window and looked up as a man passed in front of the diner. For just an instant she thought he was her mystery date from last night. Maybe the devil *was* tempting her.

"Some people believe the cards reveal hidden truths and can forecast the future by opening a channel into another world," Claire was saying as she pulled one of the plastic-covered menus from behind the condiments.

"A channel? Like HBO?" Kat asked, reaching for the other menu.

Claire laughed, the first real laugh Kat had heard out of her in years. "More like the Learning Channel." Her friend smiled. "You shouldn't be afraid of the cards. It isn't as if they're some form of sorcery."

"I'm not afraid of the cards," Kat said, sounding defensive. "But needing to know the future seems…dangerous to me."

Claire disappeared behind her menu. "Haven't you ever wondered, though, why things happen the way they do? Like if maybe there aren't some supernatural forces at work here that decide our destinies?"

Kat realized that maybe her friend needed to believe that what had happened to her was destined—and that none of them could have done anything to stop it, especially Claire herself. Five years ago Kat, Claire, Elizabeth and two other friends, Tasha Pierce and Brie Dudley, were pledging to the top sorority on campus. On a dare, they decided to spend the night in St. John's Cemetery next to McFarland Leary's grave.

As part of the hazing, one of the girls had to enter a haunted mausoleum—alone. They drew lots and Claire "won." Kat had wanted to take Claire's place, but Claire said this was something she had to do. As soon as she entered, the girls heard a scream and rushed into the mausoleum. But there was no one there.

Searchers had combed the town and the cemetery, finding no sign of Claire. Then, two days later, she miraculously turned up in the cemetery after escaping her attacker.

Kat blamed herself because she should have insisted on taking Claire's place. She could see Claire was frightened. Almost as if Claire had somehow sensed the danger. If you believed in that sort of thing. Some thought McFarland Leary had attacked Claire—a ghost. Whoever had hurt her friend was no ghost. He'd been a flesh-and-blood monster.

"You know me," Kat said now. "I have trouble believing in anything I can't see. But, wait a minute, yes, I do see a cheeseburger deluxe in my future."

Claire peeked out from behind her menu, her smile sympathetic. "You should have your cards read sometime. You might be surprised what you find out."

The last thing she wanted was to be surprised, Kat thought as she glanced through the window at Cassandra in her fortune-telling booth. "Even if I wanted to know the future, I'm not sure I could believe a woman who dressed like that," she joked, again trying to lighten the mood. When she looked at her friend, she saw Claire frowning at her.

"You had the dream again, didn't you?" Claire whispered.

Kat felt a chill. "How did you—"

"You look as if you didn't get any sleep last night." Claire shrugged. "Maybe I just know the look. I've seen it enough mornings in *my* mirror."

Kat knew that Claire had had her share of nightmares.

"Do you want to talk about it?" her friend asked. "I've learned quite a lot about dream interpretation—"

"From your friend the tarot-card reader?" Kat guessed.

Claire smiled. "Sometimes it helps if you understand what the dream is about. I have a book I'll drop by."

"I know what the dream's about," Kat said as she looked toward the window. "My mother." The moment she said the words, she wished she hadn't. Her mother was thought to have been the first victim of the serial killer who'd terrorized the town twenty years ago, and perhaps was even the same man who'd attacked Claire five years ago.

"I've often wondered why I was spared," Claire said. "I know he planned to kill me, too."

Kat didn't want to talk about this. Especially today. She knew that half the people in town, including Claire at one time, believed that the attacker had been the ghost of McFarland Leary. Kat couldn't deal with that discussion, not today. There were enough weird things going on in her world right now without digging up Leary, no pun intended.

"You said there was something you needed to talk to me about," Kat said, hoping to change the subject.

Claire nodded. "It's my little brother, Tommy. I'm worried about him. He's spending too much time with those older boys who hang out at the arcade, Razz and Dodie, and my mother is so busy with the younger children…'' Claire came from a huge family with the kids ranging in age from twenty-three to three.

Kat was very relieved Claire's request had nothing to do with ghosts or fortune-tellers. Tommy, she could handle. Tommy Cavendish was a sullen fifteen-year-old, who Kat had seen hanging out along the wharf with the boys Claire had mentioned, two locals who were always in trouble. She thought Claire probably had reason for concern.

"I think Tommy might be involved in something…illegal," Claire said quietly.

"What makes you think that?" Kat asked.

"He's so secretive and he has money, more money than a boy can make at his age running errands. I've tried to talk to him.…"

Kat nodded. "Emily doesn't listen to me either. What is it you'd like *me* to do?"

"I was hoping you would find out where Tommy's getting the money," Claire said.

Kat could see how hard it was for Claire to involve someone outside the family, even a close friend.

"I would pay you—"

"We can talk about a fee later," Kat said, not wanting to offend Claire by refusing her money, and at the same time feeling she owed her friend.

The rest of their lunch, she and Claire chatted about Elizabeth's wedding, their bridesmaid dresses and how lucky Elizabeth was after everything that had happened with the recent murders. How lucky they all were that René Rathfastar had been stopped before he killed any more young women. Moriah's Landing, they agreed, attracted weirdos.

The one man they didn't talk about was the one who was believed to have killed Kat's mother and attacked Claire. That man, whom Claire hadn't been able to identify, was still at large.

Kat noticed her friend staring across the street at the fortune-teller. "Want to tell me what Cassandra Quintana said to you?"

"She said I will find peace soon. But first I must confront my past by going back to where it all began."

"You aren't really going to go back to the cemetery based on what some fortune-teller told you, are you?"

"She knew what I'd been through," Claire said, sounding a little defensive. "I could see it in her eyes. She knew."

Sure she did. Kat wanted to tell her it didn't take psychic powers to know about Claire's attack. It had been in all the newspapers. Everyone knew. But advising her to go back to the cemetery..

"I think you should ask your doctor at the hospital about this first," Kat advised.

Claire nodded and looked toward Cassandra's booth again. "Did you notice her eyes? It was almost as if she can see *everything*."

Yes, Kat thought, remembering only too well what Cassandra had said to *her*. The seer did seem to see everything. But being observant wasn't the same as being all-knowing.

For just an instant, Kat was almost willing to pay the fortune-teller just to find out who her mystery date was, and why, since he'd come into her life, she no longer felt safe.

As Kat was paying their lunch bill, she spotted her

sister, Emily, walk past in the new bright red jacket Kat had bought her because she'd just "die" if she didn't have it. Claire's concern for her little brother, Tommy, mirrored Kat's own for her sister as she watched Emily head toward Main, then disappear into the side door of the arcade, a local hangout, and not a safe one. Also, unless Kat's watch had stopped, school wasn't out yet.

"I just saw Emily," she told Claire. "I need to talk to her. I'll see you later at Threads?" Kat and Claire were both scheduled to get their dresses fitted for Elizabeth's wedding.

"Sure," Claire said distractedly. "Thanks for lunch. You won't forget about Tommy?"

She squeezed her friend's hand. "Don't worry. I'll see what I can find out."

Emily was talking to a couple of girls from school when Kat entered the arcade. The moment her sister saw her, she looked horrified.

"Are you checking up on me?" Emily demanded in an embarrassed whisper.

"I just want to talk to you for a minute."

"Here?" Emily glanced around as if she feared everyone had seen her talking with her older sister. Heaven forbid!

"If you don't want to be seen with me, we could go outside," Kat suggested, only half-serious.

Emily took her arm and steered her out of the arcade. "That was *so* embarrassing."

"Being seen with your sister?" Kat said, trying to remember when she was a teen if she acted this weirdly.

"What do you want?"

"For starters, why aren't you in school?"

Emily rolled her eyes. "I told you last week that we were getting out early today."

Kat raised an eyebrow.

"You never believe *anything* I tell you."

Kat didn't want to argue. "I was just having lunch with Claire and I had a thought. I know you're looking for a job this summer before college." Another eye roll. "I was thinking, I could use someone to do filing and other things around my office."

"You aren't serious?" Em looked aghast.

"Well, I just thought—"

"That has to be the most *boring* job… I can find my own job, thank you. A job where I don't have you looking over my shoulder the entire time." Emily let out an exasperated sigh. "As if…" She started to turn and go back into the arcade.

"If you change your mind—"

"Yeah, right," Emily said, and disappeared back inside.

Kat stood on the sidewalk for a moment, watching her kid sister through the arcade window. She and Emily hadn't shared the same mother. But they shared some of the same problems. Emily's mother had taken off when Emily was about nine, leaving their father and Kat to finish raising the girl. Their mothers had been a lot alike, it seemed. Only, Kat's hadn't left town—just left her young daughter home with her aging grandmother so Leslie could see other men while Kat's father was at sea.

Kat went back to work but had trouble concentrating.

Still no e-mail from Ross. She couldn't keep her mind on business, her mind wandering to Claire and the fortune-teller and her mystery date. Nor could she seem to shake the uneasy feeling she'd had since last night. She remembered the devil tarot card. Temptation and fear, huh?

She glanced toward the daisies, still trying to imagine what it was about them that bothered her. All she needed was for Arabella to stop by now with another one of her warnings and her day would be complete.

Kat was almost glad for an excuse to leave the office and walk down to Threads for her fitting. The day was warm and clear, the smell of the sea mixing with all the scents of Waterfront Avenue—from the herbs and oils of the witchcraft shops to the corn dogs and cotton candy of the street vendors. There was an excitement in the air that was contagious, as if the whole town was counting down to Memorial Day weekend and the upcoming anniversary festivities.

For the first time all day, Kat felt a little better. The groups of tourists made her feel safe, the fresh air chasing away the darkness of the dream—and the events of last night. She hardly even looked for her mystery man in the faces she passed.

But half an hour later, her good mood vanished when Claire didn't show. Kat tried calling her at home. No answer. Had she decided to do what the fortune-teller had told her? Had she gone to the cemetery, a place that terrified her friend and could set back the progress she'd made?

As she left the shop, Kat realized she had just enough time to make her appointment with Bud Law-

son at his curio shop off Main. From the looks of the
place, it had obviously been kids who'd vandalized the
shop. Bud was still cleaning up when she got there.

"Any idea who they might have been?" Kat asked.

"Same ones that have been hitting all the shops,"
he said with disgust. "You can bet Dodie and Razz
were in on it, but how are you going to prove it? And
even if you could, they'll just get their hands slapped.
Someone needs to do something about those hellions."

Kat knew he had reason to be angry, but still, that
kind of talk worried her since there was no proof that
Dodie and Razz were behind the vandalism.

Back at her office, she made out her report for the
insurance company, trying to keep her mind off everything but work. It proved impossible. She found herself
calling Claire's number every hour on the hour, but still
no answer. Neither Elizabeth nor Brie had seen her.
Both told Kat not to worry. But they hadn't seen the
look on Claire's face after talking to the fortune-teller.
Did her friend want a quick cure to her pain? Who
wouldn't?

When Kat checked her e-mail, she was relieved to
see one from Ross, her real online blind date. Her relief
was short-lived when she read it though, and realized
he hadn't left the daisies.

Flowers? Me? Way too traditional. Try date
again? Witch's Brew? Coffee? Meet at your office? 7? Ross.

A man of few words. A cup of coffee at seven at
night? She thought about her mystery date last night

and the quiet, romantic window table at the Moriah's Landing Inn, and shuddered as she e-mailed Ross back:

> Seven it is. We'll meet at the Witch's Brew on Main Street, the last building before you hit the wharf. I'll be wearing jeans and a T-shirt.

He'd missed the little black dress. His loss. But she wasn't about to wear it again. In fact, she might burn the dress.

Ross had been one of those impulsive actions she hoped she wouldn't regret. She'd joined an online dating service as a fluke. Ross had sounded nice, safe, and the next thing she knew she made a date with him. She felt anxious about finally meeting. Especially after last night's imposter date and the scare he'd given her.

She turned in time to see a familiar figure passing outside her office on the other side of the street. Kat hurried out of the office to catch Tommy, and was almost to him when she saw a man in an old army jacket stop the boy on the street, show him something and then head toward her.

"Excuse me," he said, approaching her.

She just assumed he was one of the panhandlers who passed through town in the summer, bumming money for food or gas.

"Excuse me," he said, smiling, but the smile did nothing to warm his gray eyes. He had a scar on his left cheek that looked like a crescent moon. "I'm trying to find a friend of mine." He held out a snapshot in his palm. "Maybe you've seen him?"

She tried to hide her surprise as she stared at the

photo of two men, the one standing before her sans the scar on his cheek and her mystery date holding a basketball and looking hot and sweaty. Both wore shorts and T-shirts, both were tanned and in great shape, and both were smiling into the camera as if they were the best of friends.

So, Kat wondered as she looked up at the man, why didn't she believe it?

"Sorry," she said, and started to move past him.

"You're sure?" he asked, touching her arm to detain her. His tone as well as his expression seemed a little too intense, a little too desperate.

She pulled out of his reach, stepping back as she moved away from him. "I'm sure."

As she hurried after Tommy, crossing the street when he did, she realized that she should have at least asked the stranger the name of the other man in the photo. But he'd made her uncomfortable. She wondered what he wanted with her mystery date. Whatever it was, it wasn't good, she'd bet on that.

"Hi!" she said, catching up with Tommy in front of Bait & Tackle, the local bait shop.

The boy flinched as if she'd hit him. He glanced around nervously, looking guilty as hell. "Hi." He seemed to wait expectantly for her to tell him what she wanted. She'd forgotten what fifteen was like. Just as she'd forgotten seventeen, it seemed.

"I noticed you going past and I haven't seen you for a while," she said.

He nodded, still waiting.

"I saw that man stop you," she said, turning to look

back down the street. The man in the army jacket was gone. "What did he ask you?"

Tommy seemed relieved, as if she'd asked him something he didn't mind answering. "He said he was with the FBI and that he was looking for a man and had I seen him."

A different story. "Had you seen him?" she asked.

Tommy shook his head.

She realized Tommy was again waiting patiently to see what she wanted with him. "You know I have a job opening at my office for the summer, and I thought—"

"I have a job," Tommy interrupted.

"Oh, shoot, I thought you'd be great at it," she said, hoping he didn't ask what job as she glanced back down the street. She noticed Alyssa Castor, the daughter of the owner of Madam Fleury's—Yvette Castor. Alyssa appeared to be window-shopping—and tailing Tommy.

Kat saw the girl's expression as she stole a look at Tommy. Kat recognized the look: idol worship. It appeared Alyssa had a major crush and, as always seemed to be the case, he didn't even know she was alive—let alone following him.

"So where are you working?" Kat asked conversationally, watching a few tourists mingle past.

"I'm just running errands for a few guys," Tommy said, sounding both defensive and evasive, two sure giveaways, if there were any.

"Em's looking for a job." She hoped. "Errands, huh? Here, along Waterfront?"

He squirmed a little. "Just for Ernie here at Bait &

Tackle and Brody at the Wharf Rat and some other guys.''

She nodded, trying to imagine what errands someone like Brody at the Wharf Rat—a bar—would have for a fifteen-year-old boy. Alyssa had stopped a door behind them pretending to admire a huge gargoyle in one of the witch-shop windows. "Maybe you could run errands for me, too."

He shrugged. "I'm pretty busy already, you know."

She didn't know, but she planned to find out. "So what type of errands could I maybe get you to do for me? If you had time? Get me lunch? Or take packages to the post office? What do you do for the other guys?"

Before Tommy could answer, loud angry voices erupted from the bar in question. An instant later, a man came flying out of the bar's front door as if thrown. He stumbled and fell to the bricks, followed quickly by another.

"Take it outside," a third man called after them, flinging the cap of one of the men to the ground. The first man stumbled to his feet and dived at the second man still on the bricks. The two began wrestling awkwardly, obviously having had way too much to drink.

What caught and held her attention weren't the quarreling drunks, but the man who'd just thrown the pair out of the bar. She stared at her mystery date from the night before, wondering why she was so shocked to see that he worked at the Wharf Rat. No wonder she'd been attracted to him! The man was an obvious loser—which unfortunately was her type of late. Maybe someone from the FBI really *was* looking for him.

He looked up, meeting her gaze, and she quickly

swung back around to Tommy, disgusted with herself for being attracted to the wrong type, but also feeling relieved he wasn't some psychopath just passing through town whom she'd not only had dinner with but had almost kissed.

When she turned, however, Tommy was gone. So was Alyssa. Angry that she'd let Tommy get away so easily, she crossed the street and started toward her office—and tripped over nothing, pitching headlong toward the brick pavement.

Chapter Four

"Hello." Jonah caught her in his arms. Had he tripped her? He couldn't believe it. Not when he'd promised himself he'd keep his distance from her. But that seemed damned impossible in a town the size of Moriah's Landing. Even if he'd wanted to.

She looked surprised—either that she'd tripped on seemingly nothing but thin air—or that he'd rushed in to catch her with such quickness. She also looked a little suspicious. Imagine that.

She shook herself free of him, dark blue eyes sparking with anger and a little fear. "I'm sorry, do I know you?" Oh that mouth. He desperately regretted having not kissed her last night.

It was obvious she'd found out about their "date." He scanned the small crowd that had gathered around the brawling drunks, but he didn't see anyone he knew in the faces. "Sorry about last night," he said, turning his attention back to Kat. "Not sorry about the date. Just that I didn't mention, I wasn't *him*. My name's Jonah." He held out his hand.

She ignored it. "You took advantage of the situation."

He smiled. "That I did."

"You aren't in the least bit sorry, are you?" she snapped, and started to turn away.

He caught her arm and leaned close to her ear, the scent in her dark hair intoxicating. "The only thing I *regret* is that I didn't kiss you when I had the chance."

"You blew your chance," she snapped, pulling free of him. "And since you won't be around long, with the FBI looking for you…"

He caught her by the wrist. "What did you say?"

"A man who said he's an agent from the FBI is showing your picture around town, asking if anyone knows how he can find you."

Deke Turner. Damn. "What did he look like?"

"Stocky, with gray eyes and a small crescent-shaped scar—"

He swore and released her. Definitely Deke. Definitely the man he'd recognized in the fog last night. The same man who'd recognized him—just before Jonah ducked inside Kat's office.

"So you do know him." Did she sound disappointed?

"Yeah."

"Then you'll be leaving town," she said, looking way too hopeful. So that's why she'd warned him about Deke.

He could still feel the warmth of her wrist between his fingers even though he was no longer touching her. Just as he could still sense something around her like a bad aura. "You suppose wrong." He couldn't leave now, even if he wanted to.

"Too bad," she said, and walked away.

He stared after her, still shocked by what he'd felt when he'd touched her and angry with himself for feeling anything. He blamed it on being back in this town. But unlike last night when he'd felt only an ominous presence around her, today he'd definitely detected something much stronger, much more dangerous.

Kat Ridgemont was in some kind of trouble. He could feel it. And if there was one thing he knew, it was trouble.

He considered going after her, trying to warn her. Yeah, like Arabella had last night?

"I see danger in your future," a woman said behind him.

He turned to find the fortune-teller leaning against the wall, watching him from her dark hooded eyes.

"And I see dead people," he answered, stealing a line from a movie.

"You will see a lot more if you aren't careful." With that, she pushed off the wall and disappeared back into her booth, her jewelry jangling after her.

He shook his head as he went back inside the bar. As if he didn't have enough problems, now he had a damn fortune-teller telling him things he already knew.

His biggest concern right now, though, was Deke. No, he thought, it was not getting involved in whatever trouble Kat Ridgemont was in. He didn't need more trouble. He had enough of his own. But he couldn't forget the feeling he had when he was around her any more than he could forget her. Both a problem.

"I think you've finally found your calling," the owner of the Wharf Rat jeered as Jonah stepped behind the bar again. Brody Ries straddled a stool at the far end, a cigar hanging from his thick lips, his small brown eyes narrowed against the smoke spiraling up. "You seem to have a real talent for mean-drunk tossing."

"You might be right, cuz," Jonah said, hiding his irritation, which alone was a full-time job.

"Maybe getting kicked out of the FBI was the best thing that could have happened to you," Brody said, and laughed, never one to pass up the opportunity to kick a man when he was down. "Working for me, you get to learn about *real* life. Not like that fancy-ass school you went to, I can sure as hell tell you that."

Brody had always resented the fact that Jonah had gotten a scholarship his freshman year in high school to go to Wentworth Academy in Boston. It was there that he'd put his past behind him. Moriah's Landing. His family. And all that both meant to him. He'd never looked back, going on to college and then getting into the FBI. If he'd had his way, he'd have never come back here.

But plans change.

"You know, it's odd," Brody was saying, "one of your old buddies was in here just last night, not two hours before you showed up. An ex-FBI agent by the name of Deke Turner. Ring any bells?"

Just that loud clanging one that reminded him how dead he was if he ran into Deke again. "Maybe, but then the FBI is kind of a large place, you know, Brody."

"Oh yeah?" Brody looked disappointed. And skeptical. "Too bad. You two have a lot in common. It seems he got booted out of the FBI, too. Only, I would have sworn he said he knew you. What's wild is that he said he just got out of the slammer and heard about your trouble with the feds and decided to come looking for you. Seems he just missed you. Maybe he'll come back in today.''

Jonah busied himself behind the bar, trying to keep from looking toward the door and letting Brody see just how worried he was about Deke showing up right now.

"So, what exactly are you going to teach me, Brody?'' he asked, trying to keep his tone light, trying to change the subject.

"Oh, you'll see, *cuz*. We'll see how you do behind the bar first.'' He studied him. "I'll be watching you *real* close. The only reason I'm trusting you at all is because we are blood.''

Don't remind me, Jonah thought. I'll be watching you even closer, *cuz*. He'd seen Brody's expensive sports car, the fancy clothes, heard about the ostentatious home outside of town, the money-hungry ex-wife and the semiclassy influential friends, all out of Brody's league. Either the bar made a *lot* of money and Brody's manners had improved, or his cousin was into something dishonest but highly profitable. Jonah would bet on the latter.

"I can't tell you what your giving me a job means to me,'' he said honestly. The Wharf Rat was the heartbeat of the wharf area. Something illegal going on? This was the place to find out. Brody had his fingers in anything and everything—including a poker game with a man Jonah was dying to meet.

"We've all been down on our luck,'' Brody said,

still eyeing him. "But all the way from an FBI agent to barkeep, that's one long fall."

He'd expected Brody to be suspicious—and he was. Jonah would have to watch himself. His cousin was no fool.

"Even you, it seems, can hit the bottom of the barrel," Brody said, as if in awe. "Maybe if you play your cards right, you won't always have to be a bartender."

Jonah was counting on it.

BACK AT HER OFFICE, Kat took out her frustrations doing the job she hated most: filing, which included kicking a few file cabinets and slamming a few drawers.

Her face still burned, Jonah's words still buzzing in her ears, the memory of his touch branding her skin with a fire his words had done little to put out.

She was totally disgusted with herself.

She couldn't believe she'd felt relieved to find out he had a job in town and wasn't just some drifter passing through. Right now she'd love to see his backside heading out on the highway.

Especially since she hadn't missed his reaction when she told him about the "FBI friend" asking about him. As if it wasn't bad enough that he was a bartender at the Wharf Rat, she suspected that wasn't even the worst of it.

Digging into the huge stack of filing, she reminded herself of her plan to get a receptionist. The problem was, every time she thought about hiring someone, something came up. This time, it was a new furnace for the house. She also wanted to help with Emily's tuition in the fall. Kat was determined that girl was going to college. If not Heathrow, then somewhere else.

Their father had left them both insurance money, but it wouldn't be enough if Emily got into a good college. Kat had been given the greater share because their father had known she would have to finish raising Emily if anything happened to him. Emily wouldn't get the bulk of her inheritance until she turned twenty-one, which had become a sore point with her sister.

"Daddy didn't trust me," Em had cried.

"I'm sure he just thought you would appreciate the money more when you finished college."

Her sister had given her one of those eye-rolling looks. "I'd appreciate it right now since I'm not going to college."

Kat hadn't pushed it, but she wanted more than anything for her little sister to get an education. Em didn't have any idea how much fun college could be. But Kat did. Her best friend, Elizabeth, could attest to the good times they'd had. Kat had taught her to loosen up and Elizabeth had taught Kat how to study—the only reason Kat had gotten her degree. Elizabeth had also encouraged her to go into criminology and open an agency with the money Kat's father had left her. It had been the best two things Kat had ever done.

To her surprise, it was almost seven by the time she finished the filing. She walked to the Witch's Brew to finally meet Ross, her real online blind date, hoping he'd make her forget all about her mystery date from the night before.

JONAH CLIMBED UP the back stairs to his apartment over the bar, checking to make sure no one had been inside since he'd left. He knew Brody had a spare key and had come in while he was gone this morning. No doubt to look around for proof that Jonah was as down on his luck as he'd said.

But this time, the short piece of dental floss he'd left out of habit in the door was still in place and the second-story windows were still locked. He knew nothing had been touched as he glanced around, a deep gut knowing. The intensity of the feeling scared him, making him only too aware what being back in Moriah's Landing was doing to him. Another cause for concern.

The apartment looked worse than it had last night—and that was saying a lot. Last night he'd been too exhausted to care if it resembled a Dumpster—it already smelled like one. The moment he'd opened the door with the key his cousin had given him, he caught the entrenched scent of long-ago fried fish and spilled beer. The plasterboard walls had holes in them the shape of fists, a sure sign of what kind of renters had been here before him.

The place was small. Just a studio, with the orange shag carpet of a lost bad era, a lumpy stained gold couch that doubled as a bed, two mismatched kitchen chairs with bent legs, an ancient metal table with unimaginative graffiti carved in the top and a makeshift kitchen with a fridge that ran all the time.

The bathroom was so small he could barely turn around. It contained only a toilet and a standing metal shower stall. No sink. But as Brody said, ''There's a sink in the kitchen, and hell, it's better than living on the street, right?''

Jonah would have much preferred the street. But living over the bar fit better into his plans. He closed the blinds and reached under the couch, pushing aside the ripped underlining for the thin shelf he'd attached to the frame. Carefully he withdrew the small, state-of-the-art laptop he'd sneaked in early this morning with the groceries, and booted it up.

Last night he'd been anxious to get on the computer, but Brody had kept him up most of the night, giving him the third degree about his expulsion from the FBI. Then he'd had his first shift at the bar early this morning, no doubt just so Brody could search his room.

Anxiously, he now typed in his access number, waited for the satellite online connection, then found himself typing ''The *Landing Gazette,* archives, obit, Ridgemont.''

He told himself he was just curious. Kat said she was three when her mother died. If the mother had died in Moriah's Landing... A list of obituaries for Ridgemonts appeared on the screen. Only four were female, two were much too old to have been Kat's mother, the third too young. He brought up the fourth obit, startled by what he saw. Kat was the spitting image of her mother, Leslie Ridgemont, at the same age.

But that wasn't the only thing that shocked and scared him. Kat's mother had been murdered.

He clicked back to the archives and called up the stories on the murder, becoming more intrigued and worried as he read. The body had been found in the gazebo just feet from the witch-hanging tree on the town green—and only yards from the house where Kat lived.

A chill washed over him. The twentieth anniversary of Leslie Ridgemont's death was only days away. He didn't need to check the *Farmer's Almanac* to know that the moon would be full on that night—just as it had on the night of her death.

He swore. Some people in Moriah's Landing believed the vengeful dead rose from their graves on the first full moon. Others swore it was on the anniversary of their deaths. When he'd left town, he'd put those kinds of beliefs behind him. But he couldn't shake a bad feeling that Leslie Ridgemont was anything but gone and buried for good.

Twenty years ago. He tried to remember. He would have been eight that summer but it wasn't likely that he'd forget a murder everyone was talking about. In the newspaper articles, it said Leslie Ridgemont worked as a waitress at the Beachway Diner, so that meant his family might have known her.

The more he thought about it, the more he recalled the hushed discussions and the rumors that ran rampant throughout Moriah's Landing. Half the town blamed McFarland Leary, out of his grave and on a killing spree. But then the rumors had quickly changed to a vampire killer on the loose in the town green.

During his time at the FBI, Jonah had learned that some little thing usually got a rumor started—and that that thing often had a grain of truth. So what would have started talk of a killer vampire, especially when according to the news reports, Leslie Ridgemont had been strangled?

He reread the article, struck by how few details the press actually had. But one fact leaped out at him. The body had been discovered by Arabella Leigh. The crazy woman who'd accosted him and Kat on the street last night.

He read the rest of the stories, learning little more. Leslie Ridgemont had been strangled with a white silk scarf she'd been wearing earlier that evening. Her purse was full of change from the tips she'd made working that night at the diner, ruling out robbery. No sexual assault, but she had put up a struggle.

Reminding himself that this had nothing to do with him, Jonah found himself going through the list of possible suspects based on people who'd been seen on the town green at the time of the murder—or in close proximity.

It had been a stormy spring night, a night when the moon was full, but still the list was fairly long: his cousin, Brody Ries, high-school dropout, then age seventeen; Geoffrey Pierce, one of the town's leading residents and a would-be scientist who never made the grade, then age twenty-five; Ernie McDougal, owner of the Bait & Tackle, forty-six; Marley Glasglow, high-school dropout, fifteen; and Arabella Leigh, seamstress, sixty-seven.

The last name on the list caught Jonah's attention. Dr. Leland Manning, promising geneticist, then age thirty-five. Manning, at the time, had only recently moved back to the old Manning place due to his father's death and was building a modern, high-tech lab on his property. He'd been driving by when he'd seen the commotion at the gazebo, according to the newspaper.

An odd mix of suspects. None really had alibis, since Leslie Ridgemont was killed just moments before Arabella found her. Arabella's scream brought the others.

They'd all reported seeing each other—but no one else. The killer had never been caught, Jonah noted. Why did that worry him after all this time?

An instant-message box flashed on the screen with the words: "About time I heard from you."

"I've been busy," he typed, and hit send. He could see his boss dressed in one of her charcoal-gray pinstripe suits, sitting at her desk, ramrod straight, looking like an old-time schoolteacher. Or a nun.

"Everything fine?"

Jonah looked around the apartment. "Dandy."

"Heard from our anonymous source. We're looking for a boat called the *Audrey Lynn.*"

Jonah knew that their online transmissions were encrypted so no one could intercept them, but still he felt jumpy. Probably because the anonymous notes the FBI had received made him nervous. And damned suspicious.

"Still no idea what's on the boat?" Jonah typed, convinced he was on a fool's errand in a place that could get him killed. It had already possibly gotten another agent killed, Max Weathers. And now Jonah found himself interested in Leslie Ridgemont's murder—and feeling things he didn't want to feel about her daughter.

"No. Still having reservations?"

That was an understatement. Jonah cursed the vague

anonymous tip that had him back in Moriah's Landing. All he knew was that a boat was coming in sometime soon. It was suspected to be bringing in illegal medical supplies of some sort for someone in a secret society of scientists working out of Moriah's Landing, a society as old as the town itself and its members all secret.

But this wasn't the first boat to bring in such a shipment. Another boat had come in a month ago. Another agent had been on the case. Now that agent was missing, presumed dead, leaving Jonah to worry what had been on that boat.

"What about scientists at Heathrow College?" she wrote.

"I'll rattle their cages tomorrow." He wasn't optimistic.

"Word is the *Audrey Lynn* won't dock until end of the month," she wrote.

He swore. End of the month? He'd planned to be long gone by the full moon and that was only days away.

"Seen Dr. Manning yet?" appeared on the screen.

"Might have way to meet him. Need some poker tips though." He knew Dr. Manning played in a private weekly poker game put on by Jonah's cousin Brody. Brody had already hinted that Jonah might get lucky and be invited. Brody knew a mark when he saw one.

"Tips how to win?" she typed.

"How to lose big."

"Need more money?"

He smiled to himself. "Not yet." He thought about his most imminent problem, one of many, but the one he'd called her about last night—former FBI agent Deke Turner. Deke had recognized him even in the fog last night just before Jonah ducked into Kat's, and it seemed he was asking around town about him. Just what Jonah needed right now, a psycho like Deke Turner dogging his trail.

"Gotta have Deke out of my hair before boat comes in." If the boat existed. He couldn't help worrying that someone might have purposely gotten him back to Moriah's Landing knowing full well just how dangerous it could be for him.

"Picked him up. Can only hold him forty-eight hours though. Sorry."

"That will have to do." In just over seventy-two hours the moon would be full and Jonah planned to be miles from this town by then. At least he'd better be.

"Remember. Officially, you have no net."

"Or rules." In order to cover his ass, the FBI had booted him—at least on paper.

"You're there just to find out what happened to Max, not to avenge his death."

That was assuming he was dead, which they all thought he was.

Jonah stared at the screen, feeling a wave of guilt. He should have taken the assignment when it was offered to him. He shouldn't have let Max Weathers come to Moriah's Landing without knowing just what he was up against. But even as he thought it, Jonah knew he couldn't have warned Max about Moriah's Landing and Jonah's own history there. And even if he had, Max would never have believed him.

"Anything else?" she typed.

As a matter of fact... "Need copy of a local murder file."

The screen stayed empty for a few moments.

"Connected to assignment?"

"Possibly." It wasn't really a lie.

"What name?"

"Leslie Ridgemont."

UNFORTUNATELY FOR KAT, her online blind date turned out to be exactly what she'd originally expected—a computer nerd complete with Coke-bottle-thick glasses and a pocket protector.

Unlike her date from the night before, he talked about nothing else *but* himself, telling her a lot more about his abilities with computers and the Internet than she'd ever wanted to know. Too bad he wasn't the man of few words he'd been online.

And, of course, he'd tried to kiss her as they left the Witch's Brew. Just her luck.

After saying goodbye—for good—to Ross, Kat had called home. No answer. Restless and hoping she'd see her sister, Emily, she walked down Waterfront Avenue. Sometime over her third cup of coffee with the incredibly boring Ross, she'd decided she couldn't go on being afraid. She had never run from Moriah's Landing or her family's history here and she wasn't going to let some stranger in town intimidate her.

One way to do that was to find out everything there was to know about Jonah—including his last name. After all, she was an investigator. But she was also smart enough to know just how dangerous learning more about him might be—in more ways than one.

She couldn't help but remember that her uneasiness had begun last night *before* she'd learned he wasn't her real date.

At the same time, she couldn't deny that he thrilled her. She'd known last night that he was dangerous. Dangerous to her because he was just the kind of man she shouldn't be attracted to.

But was that the only danger she had to fear from this man? She needed to know why he'd pretended to be her date. She also needed to know who had left the daisies. Not Ross, who denied sending them. That left her mystery date. And that other set of footsteps she'd heard following her last night.

At the end of the street, the hulking remains of the old abandoned cannery loomed up. Music drifted from the bars and shops, mixing in a cacophony of excited sounds as the first wave of tourists wandered the streets, picking up local color and curios, hoping to see a present-day witch or scare themselves with the stories of Leary's ghost or a visit to the cemetery late at night.

Unlike the night before, the evening was clear, the almost full moon golden above the treetops. Out over the water, though, mist rose ghostlike among the boats moored there.

Kat had always loved this time of year in Moriah's Landing. She didn't even mind the tourists or all the witchcraft fanfare when shop owners dressed as witches and a hearse cruised the drag, offering cemetery tours. In the winter, the town seemed to hunker down against the nor'easters that moved up the coast bringing wind, rain and even snow.

She liked the feeling that anything could happen this

time of year, and she'd never felt it more than she did tonight, a tingling mixture of excitement and fear as she neared the Wharf Rat.

"Why, hello."

She turned, startled and yet ridiculously hopeful, as she followed the sound of the voice into the shadows at the edge of the building. But the voice was all wrong. So was the face.

Marley Glasglow stepped from the deep shadows into the light, a misanthropic sneer below the brim of his dirty straw hat. He was a big, burly, ill-tempered man who made no secret of his dislike of women.

"Oh? Did I disappoint you?" His lips curled. Not a smile. Nor was the sound he made a laugh. "What? You were expecting someone else? Maybe the new bartender? Sorry, Jonah already left."

She realized that Glasglow must have seen her earlier today when she was talking to her mystery date in front of the Wharf Rat. Glasglow worked for the bait shop's owner, Ernie McDougal.

She started to walk on past the bar—and Glasglow, too stubborn to let him think he intimidated her.

"Did he tell you he was kicked out of the FBI?"

Marley must have seen her surprise. He let out a snort. "You sure are your mother's daughter, aren't you?"

The words stunned her as sharp and hurtful as a slap. Before she could respond, he was swallowed up again in shadow, the sound of his footfalls retreating between the buildings. Then a door opened at the back of the Wharf Rat and Marley disappeared inside.

Kat hugged herself from the chill the man had left

behind. She wanted to yell after him that he was dead wrong about her. But she was too upset by what he'd said about her—and about her mystery blind date. Kicked out of the FBI? Maybe the man in the army coat hadn't been lying after all. She could really pick 'em, that was for sure.

She stood for a moment, scrubbing her original plan to go into the Wharf Rat and try to find out more about Jonah. She didn't want to see Marley again. Nor did she like the sound of raised voices inside the bar. And hadn't she found out more than enough about Jonah already?

Behind her she could hear the sound of waves as a boat came into the cove. But it was something closer that drew her attention—the sound of paint coming out of an aerosol-spray can.

She crossed the street, working her way past the dark, empty bait shop to the corner of the building where she could see the wharf with its huge weathered dark pilings stark against the water and mist. She could hear the spray cans and the whisper of voices as she edged closer, deeper into the dark.

From across the street, the front door of the Wharf Rat banged open and a couple of men came out, both talking loudly. The sound of the spray cans stopped abruptly. Kat hurried around the corner of the building just in time to see three figures running away, headed north past the old cannery.

She knew she'd never be able to catch the vandals, not in the platform sandals she had on—even if she'd been able to move. Instead, she watched the three escape, too shocked to take even a step. One of the vandals was small and definitely female, her hair dark and shoulder-length. The girl was wearing a bright new red jacket, exactly like the one Kat had bought for Emily, the one she just had to have.

Chapter Five

Another sound made her spin around, jumpy now and suddenly aware how dark it was this close to the wharf and how alone she was. A fourth figure moved along the rocky shore of the cove, seemingly unable to move quickly. A fourth vandal?

Kat slipped along the back edge of the building, staying in the dark shadow of the wall until she was close enough to recognize him. Tommy Cavendish.

At first she thought the boy was hurt and that's why he hadn't been able to run with the others. Then she heard the clink of the glass bottle in his hand as he caught himself on the rocks. He raised the bottle to his lips, tilted his head back and took a long swig, then staggered forward. Tommy was drunk, falling-down plastered!

Before she could move, she saw a second person drop over the short seawall toward Tommy. Hanging back, she watched the all-too-familiar man as he approached the boy. She had a pretty good idea where Tommy had gotten the alcohol, which made her so angry she almost stormed down there to confront them both.

"Give me that," Jonah ordered the boy, taking the bottle and pouring the remainder of the booze onto the rocks as he helped Tommy back up to the seawall. "Sit."

Tommy sat, Jonah joining him, their backs to her, just feet away. It was clear the two knew each other, but she wasn't so sure now that Jonah had supplied the boy the liquor.

"I don't feel so good," Tommy said, his head falling between his knees.

"I would imagine not," Jonah said. "And just think, you're going to feel even worse in the morning." He put his hand on the boy's back as Tommy heaved onto the rocks at his feet. "I suppose we all have to learn about alcohol the hard way. I know I did." Kat had, too.

"Why does something that makes you feel so good make you feel so bad?" Tommy groaned in between fits of vomiting.

The older male chuckled. "A lot of things in life are that way until you come to understand the word *moderation.*" He handed the boy his handkerchief.

Kat felt sorry for Tommy and angry with him at the same time. She watched Jonah, surprised at the caring, sympathetic way he helped the boy.

"Thanks," Tommy said, and wiped his mouth as he glanced sideways at the man next to him.

"That wasn't you vandalizing the back side of Ernie's bait shop, was it?" Jonah asked.

Tommy shook his head. The movement seemed to make the boy sick again. It was pretty obvious he was too drunk to do much damage—except to himself.

"But you know who they were," Jonah said.

Tommy didn't raise his head. "It was too dark to make them out." It was an obvious lie.

"Then I guess there's no chance I'll see you running with them," Jonah said.

"I heard you were looking for a boat," Tommy said in an obvious change of subject.

Kat felt her heart rate kick up. She leaned against the wall, her interest piqued.

"A boat called the *Audrey Lynn?*"

"That's right," he said, looking at the boy. "You've seen it?"

Tommy shook his head.

"If you do, I'd appreciate if you'd let me know. I'd make it worth your while."

"Are you thinking of hiring on?"

"You never know," Jonah said.

Kat couldn't see him hiring on to any boat and wondered what his interest was in it as she watched him help Tommy to his feet.

"Think you're up to going home now?" he asked the boy.

"Are you going to tell on me?" Tommy asked, sounding scared. "It's just that my sister worries about me too much." As if Claire had no reason to worry.

"I won't say anything to your sister. But if I catch you drinking again or even near any vandals, I'm going to kick your butt myself and save your sister the effort."

"I'm never drinking again," Tommy groaned.

"Yeah, right. Now get out of here."

As Tommy slipped off the seawall and stumbled up

Waterfront Avenue toward home, Kat stepped back, watching Jonah as he got up and headed down the wharf.

She told herself there was no reason to follow him. She'd learned enough about him for one night. But of course she did follow him.

The mist on the water had grown thicker, the air colder and damp. She moved along the wharf toward the docks where boats rocked gently at their moorings. Where was he going? He moved as if he had some purpose in mind. Not like a man out for a walk, especially on a dock that specifically said Only Boat Owners Beyond This Point.

Maybe he owned a boat. Yeah, right.

She could hear the foghorn at the lighthouse. Closer, water lapped softly against the sides of the boats moored in the cove. She caught glimpses of boats through wisps of fog as she moved quietly along the dock. Where had Jonah gone? She couldn't see him ahead of her anymore. It would be just her luck to come face-to-face with him in the thick mist. Or worse, crash into him and find herself in the water.

She froze as she heard a sound close by. The whoosh of something moving through water, then a dripping sound, followed by another whoosh, then dripping. It took her only a moment to recognize what was making the noise. Someone was rowing a boat away from the dock just yards ahead of her.

She stopped motionless to listen, staring into the shimmering fog, then moved down the dock past the quiet boats until she caught a glimpse through the mist.

Jonah was rowing a small dinghy out to one of the

fishing boats moored in the cove, his back muscles bunching as he pulled on the oars.

What was he up to? He stopped rowing and started to turn. She ducked back behind the bow of the boat she'd been hiding behind just an instant before he saw her. Holding her breath, she listened for the sound of the oars cutting through the water again.

Even when she heard him begin to row again, she waited. The fog whirled around her, cold and wet. She should be home in bed. What did she care what this man was up to? After a moment, she peeked around the edge of the bow and saw that Jonah had reached the fishing boat.

He tossed up a rope ladder and climbed aboard stealthily. She watched, half expecting him to get caught. But then who else was out on a night like this? Just the two of them, it appeared.

She waited, wondering what he was doing on the boat. Looking for something to steal? A few moments later, he appeared again, swung down over the side and dropped back into the dinghy, snapping the ladder loose as if he'd done this sort of things hundreds of times. He probably had.

As far as she could tell, he hadn't taken anything from the fishing boat—at least nothing large.

She stayed out of sight, listening to him row back toward her, realizing she should have left the moment she saw him get back into the dinghy. Now she was trapped. If she moved down the dock, he was bound to see her. And she wanted to avoid him at all costs.

Suddenly she realized that the rowing sound had stopped. The dinghy banged softly into the dock just yards from her. She felt the wood creak under Jonah's weight as he climbed out.

She hunkered down, assured where she was in the dark shadow of a large boat's bow, that he wouldn't see her as he passed. She was debating whether or not she should follow him once he was back on shore when she realized she hadn't heard him since he'd gotten out of the dinghy. Nor could she feel him coming. She held her breath, closing her eyes, willing him to get past.

"Hello?" he said, his voice deep, setting something inside her vibrating.

She jumped, her eyes flying open, to find him standing over her. How had he known she was there? He stood only a few inches from her and yet she hadn't heard him approach. The man moved like a cat.

Her heart leaped to her throat as her hand dropped to her shoulder bag and the Beretta inside it, out of her reach. She straightened, suddenly aware of just how completely alone they were. What was it about this man that had her so spooked?

"Sorry, didn't mean to scare you," he said, holding his palms up in mock surrender.

"Did I say you scared me?" she snapped.

He moved closer until she could smell his aftershave, a heady male scent, and see his features even in the muted dock lights.

"My mistake," he said quietly, his voice sending a shiver through her, his gaze calling her a liar as surely as he was standing before her. "Lose something?"

She straightened, pulling out and palming her earring as she did, then looked down, pretending she'd dropped something on the dock. "My earring," she said, keeping her head down.

"Let me help," he said as he kneeled next to her. "What does it look like?"

"Small and silver...." He was too close. She could feel his breath stir her hair. She reached down and pretended to pluck the earring up from the weathered boards, sure he could hear her heart drumming in her chest. "I have it."

He stood again, his gaze so intent she thought it would make her burst into flames. "So you do," he said softly, his lips quirked into a mocking smile.

She squirmed, unable not to, with him this close and looking at her like that. He seemed to be waiting for her to tell him what she was really doing here. Fat chance.

She saw him look toward her hand clutching the Beretta through the leather purse. She relaxed her grip. And yet she felt as if she was risking a lot more than her life standing out here alone with him.

He smiled, obviously amused, as if he could hear the frantic pounding of her heart and knew exactly why it beat so fast, so hard.

"You're still mad about last night," he said.

Is that what he thought? "You mean because I went to dinner with a man whose name I don't even know?"

"Jonah. Remember?"

She already knew that much—and a whole lot more, thanks to Marley Glasglow. She waited for a second name but it appeared one wasn't coming. "Just Jonah?"

A muscle in his jaw jumped. "Jonah...Ries," he said, his tone challenging.

"Ries?" She couldn't hide her shock. "You aren't related to—"

"Brody's my cousin, not that either of us admit it willingly. Or claim any connection to the rest of the family."

Ries. At least that explained why he hadn't wanted to tell her his last name. Could it get any worse? So what was she doing still standing here?

"Last night I was telling you about the town," she heard herself saying. "And you know more than I do. After all, your family's been here longer than mine." She cringed, remembering how she told him about McFarland Leary and his witch, both rumored to have been ancestors of the Ries family.

She felt herself getting angry again—at him for being deceitful, at herself for falling for it. She now not only knew what he was, but who he was. So why didn't she just turn tail and run?

Because, blast the man to hell, she kept picturing him with Tommy on the shore, handing the boy a handkerchief and telling him he'd kick his butt if he caught him drinking again. Why didn't that fit with what she knew about Jonah Ries?

Jonah said nothing, his face granite still.

"You couldn't have grown up here," she said, thinking out loud. The town was too small; she'd have known him.

"I left my freshman year in high school," he said, narrowing his gaze at her. "Let's see, that would have made you about...eight or nine?"

That could explain why she didn't remember him. That and the fact that the Rieses all lived on the wrong side of town and kept to themselves. Talk about weird families. They gave new meaning to the word *dysfunctional.*

"Look, for what it's worth, I really am sorry about last night," he said, and glanced down the deserted dock. "You never did say what you were doing out here this late at night."

He knew damn well that she'd followed him. She'd bet on that. "I couldn't sleep. What are you doing here?"

"I couldn't sleep either." He kept looking at her with that same I-can-lie-as-well-as-you-can expression on his handsome face. "So we have that in common, too."

"Too? I can't imagine what else we could have in common."

"We're both from Moriah's Landing and we both have insatiable curiosities," he said smoothly.

"Do we?"

He smiled then. "So it would seem." He looked past her as if he could see through the fog—maybe he had X-ray vision. Maybe that's how he'd known she was hiding on the dock. "Is there someplace in town that's open this time of night where we could get warm milk for you? I hate to see you lose any sleep."

"Thanks, but I'm practically dozing off on my feet now." She started past him. He caught her arm.

"I don't like seeing you out this late at night alone," he said.

She would just bet he didn't. Hopefully, next time

he *wouldn't* see her. If there was a next time. "Thanks for your concern, but I can take care of myself." His fingers felt as if they might burn her skin.

He let go of her arm. "I sure hope so."

She didn't like the way he said it, almost like a threat. For some reason, it made her think of the daisies. "By the way," she said, sidestepping him, wanting to run because, as much as she denied it, something about him pulled at her like the moon on the tide, "next time you leave flowers on a woman's doorstep, leave a card."

He raised an eyebrow.

Her heart kicked up several beats as she saw the answer in his dark expression. She stopped moving. "You didn't leave a bouquet of daisies on my doorstep this morning?"

He shook his head and frowned.

"If you didn't leave them..." She was more anxious than ever to get away from him for reasons even she couldn't explain. She turned, planning to take off, but he moved too fast.

He grabbed her again, swinging her into him, one hand coming to rest at the small of her back, the other behind her head as his lips unerringly found hers.

His kiss was everything she'd imagined—and more. His mouth warm, firm, demanding, his breath stealing hers as he gave and took with equal parts passion.

She would have fought both him and the kiss, had he given her even half a chance. But he'd taken her by surprise—just as his kiss had—and left her reeling when it ended abruptly.

His gaze met hers in the glow of the street lamp as

he released her. "I hate having regrets," he said matter-of-factly, then turned and left her on the deserted dock without another word, leaving her to stare after him, the taste and feel of him still on her lips.

She cursed his black heart. It seemed he had no qualms about leaving her with one *big* regret—that she wouldn't be kissing him again.

JONAH DIDN'T GO FAR. He waited in the shadows of a building, still stinging from the look in Kat's eyes when he'd told her his name, and still floating from the feel of his mouth on hers. Damn woman. He couldn't believe she'd followed him. Just what he needed. It was high time he did something about it. But what?

He didn't have to wait long. Kat made a beeline for home, walking fast, obviously angry and, unfortunately, completely unaware of her surroundings. Didn't she realize how dangerous that was?

For her own good, he followed her home again, angry with her, with himself. He should have been used to seeing that unpleasant reaction to the Ries name. He'd seen it often enough growing up here. He'd spent most of his almost thirty years trying to live down his family history. Away from here, it had been easy to become someone else, something else. But now that he was back, he was one of them again, whether he liked it or not.

It had taken everything in him not to try to convince her he wasn't like the other Rieses. But it would have been a lie. And he would have regretted it—unlike the kiss. Her mouth had been full and wet, pliable and sweet. And all he could think about was kissing her again.

A few clouds played hide-and-seek with the moon now hanging over town, golden and growing larger with each passing night. This far from the water, away from the fog, it was clear. Because of that, he could be fairly sure he was the only one tailing her tonight. And just as sure time was running out for him. And possibly for Kat as well.

Kissing her had only convinced him he hadn't been wrong last night. She was in danger. The feeling was too strong, as if whatever was after her was close by.

He realized he was racing the moon and howling in the darkness. He had no idea what was going on. Or what was coming in on the boat. Or what had happened to the last agent who'd come here on the same mission. But what threw him most was the feeling he got when he was around Kat.

He was going on nothing but instinct, an instinct he'd spent years trying desperately to kill. But unfortunately, you can't kill who you are, he thought bitterly, and coming back to Moriah's Landing had made that all too clear—had brought out his heritage.

The irony of the situation didn't escape him. He'd always seen his ability to "know" things as a curse. But right now he would have given anything to see the future clearer. To see Kat Ridgemont's future. And know how to save her.

Daisies. Someone had left daisies on her doorstep. What was that about? Nothing good, he was damn sure.

As he followed her at a distance through the park and town green, he thought again about trying to warn her. He'd seen the fear in her eyes tonight when he'd approached her. Now that she knew who his family was, she seemed even more afraid of him. She would have little reason to trust him, let alone believe anything he said.

She was in danger. But try to explain those instincts and what they foretold to a woman like Kat, who'd already made it clear that she didn't believe in any of that "hocus-pocus, supernatural stuff."

He'd forgotten how strong those instincts could be. But being back in Moriah's Landing, he could feel their power escalating, his body and mind becoming more and more aware as the moon grew in the velvet sky overhead.

He leaned against the trunk of a tree, hidden by the dense foliage, feeling like a stalker as he waited for Kat to go inside and lock the door behind her.

Maybe *he* was the evil he sensed around Kat. There was a thought.

He watched her disappear into her house, listened for the lock and for the lights to come on, needing assurance that she was safe. At least for tonight.

Then he moved across the damp grass, the night air salty and clear. He knew he couldn't sleep until he finished this. After reading about Kat's mother's murder, he had to see the spot. Had to test himself.

The gazebo came into view beyond the trees. His steps slowed and for a moment he wondered if this wasn't the dumbest idea he'd had yet. Slowly, he walked toward the gazebo.

A slight breeze stirred the ivy growing up the white lattice sides. He heard a groan and realized he was no longer alone. He turned quickly. Darkness pooled under the huge oak tree nearby and for just an instant he thought he saw the dark silhouettes of the witches hanging from the largest of the tree's branches, the limb groaning under their weight.

But then the leaves rustled, the limb groaned again in the breeze and the image was gone as if it had never been there.

He stood, stone still, listening to the sounds of the night, remembering everything he'd read in the FBI file that had come attached to his latest e-mail. Apparently, the local police records on the serial killings twenty years ago were missing. That left only the federal file.

Leslie Ridgemont had been found lying on her back on the far bench in the gazebo, her head hanging over the edge, the white scarf around her neck fluttering in the breeze.

The police believed that she'd known her attacker and possibly let the killer walk her home. She'd definitely let him get close enough to strangle her. But what had thrown them about the case were the two cuts on her throat near her carotid artery—a fact not released to the newspapers. But somehow the truth got out. That, Jonah knew, had started the rumor about a killer vampire on the town green.

He moved to the bench and closed his eyes, envisioning the scene that Arabella Leigh had found that night twenty years ago.

Concentrating, he recalled the photographs from the FBI file. He could see the body, the red-and-white snug-fitting diner uniform hiked up, the bare legs, no socks, spoiled white sneakers, the scarf, the cuts on the neck.

He opened his eyes with a start, his heart pounding. He'd seen it all as if it had been him finding the body instead of Arabella—except the face hadn't been Leslie Ridgemont's—it was Kat's.

He stumbled out of the gazebo, feeling weak. It wasn't just the uncanny resemblance between mother and daughter. He'd seen Kat's face on the corpse—not her mother's, and he knew, soul deep, that someone planned to put Kat on that same bench by the full moon.

Shaken to the core, he lifted his head, his gaze going straight to the three-story clapboard house as if something inside him knew—had known since the beginning.

She stood at the railing on the widow's walk wearing a white nightgown. It fluttered in the breeze as she looked out toward the sea.

He felt a shudder rattle through him as he stared at her, his heart pounding. *My God.* Had she stood in that same spot the night her mother was killed twenty years ago, Kat would have seen the murderer. But would she have remembered?

Shaken, he turned to leave. Something moved at the edge of the trees. Someone. He caught the shine of eyes, eyes that only a moment before had been doing the same thing Jonah's had—staring at Kat's house and the woman on the widow's walk. The same person who'd been following them the night before?

Jonah took off at a run toward the dark figure in the trees. That ever-growing moon slipped behind the clouds, leaving the night filled with darkness and even darker shadows. His body surged with adrenaline as he sprinted across the grass, a desperate need to stop the evil that he'd sensed was after Kat Ridgemont.

He reached the trees where he'd seen the figure, rounded the stand of oaks, but there was nothing in the cool darkness beneath the wide branches. No one.

Something on the ground caught Jonah's eye. Next to the indentation of a footprint in the grass lay what appeared to be a glove. He stooped to pick it up, only to find the rough, worn leather glove was dry and almost warm. The man he'd seen watching Kat's house had to have dropped it.

He swung around at a sound, saw a man running hell-bent toward Main Street, and went after him, knowing in every cell of his body that the person he chased would eventually hurt Kat if he didn't stop him.

It wasn't until he crossed Main Street that Jonah realized where the person was headed. St. John's Cemetery, where McFarland Leary was buried. He could make out the tangled web of tree limbs, the dark jagged lines of the wrought-iron fence, the headstones glowing in the moonlight. Jonah felt his feet falter.

That moment's hesitation was all it took. He sprinted across Main and up the brick sidewalk along the edge of the cemetery, but by the time he reached the huge wrought-iron gate at the entrance, he knew it was too late. From the back of the cemetery, Jonah heard a car engine turn over, then the grinding of gears and the spray of gravel as the car sped off west of town and out of his view.

Jonah swore, bent to catch his breath, his hands on

his thighs, head down. In front of him was the gate to the cemetery. The gate to his own personal hell. He straightened and gazed through the twisted wrought iron, through the misshapen branches of the dark trees to where McFarland Leary lay restless in his grave, the stone stark white in the light from the moon.

"Not tonight, Leary." Jonah took a couple of steps backward, heart pounding, his muscles suddenly weak as seawater. "Not tonight, you son of a bitch."

Then he turned his back to the graves and headed toward the tiny apartment he was renting from his cousin Brody over the Wharf Rat. Home.

For the first time since he'd walked out of the FBI headquarters at Quantico, he felt as if he really had hit rock bottom.

Chapter Six

Kat woke with a cry of anguish, her legs tangled in the sheets, her skin clammy with fear. She fought to free herself of the sheets, of the nightmare, surprised it was morning, and worse, that she'd overslept.

Grabbing her robe, she stumbled down the stairs, following the smell of coffee. Emily had made a pot before she'd left for school. But why hadn't Em at least tried to wake her? Maybe she had.

With a groan, Kat remembered last night and the girl in the red jacket she'd seen running away after vandalizing the Bait & Tackle wall. As much as she dreaded it, she'd have to confront Em tonight about it since the girl hadn't been home by the time Kat had fallen asleep.

Kat poured herself some coffee and stood barefoot in the kitchen, her hands wrapped around the warm cup, trying to eradicate the chill inside her. She couldn't forget about the dream. It had come back just as she'd feared, only this time…this time it had been different. She shuddered at the vague memory and took a sip of the hot liquid. The strong coffee did little to melt away the block of ice inside her, though.

Taking the cup with her, Kat headed for the stairs and a shower. But as she started up the steps, she spotted a book on the lower step near the front door. *Dream Interpretation: Unlock the Mystery.*

But it was the note stuck to the front cover from Claire that made Kat pick up the book.

Hi. Sorry I blew you off at Threads. Didn't mean to worry you. Just lost track of time. Call you tomorrow, Claire.

Relieved that Claire was okay, Kat carried the book upstairs. She started to drop it on her desk when, on impulse, she thumbed through the pages, expecting to find something funny she could tell Elizabeth about. Elizabeth had been so busy getting ready for the wedding they hadn't talked much lately and Kat figured they both could use a good laugh.

A word caught her eye, suddenly bringing back the dream with such force that her knees threatened to buckle. She clutched the edge of the desk for a moment. She'd seen something new in the dream last night, something she'd never seen before in the bizarre jumble of images, something she'd remembered. Slowly, she opened the book to the word that had triggered the memory.

Blood: Seeing blood in a dream indicates enemies who seek to destroy you. Beware of someone close to you who isn't who you think they are.

Ridiculous. Kat slammed the book shut and dropped it on her desk. If only it were that easy to shed the dream, she thought as she went to shower and get ready for work.

AT THE SAME TIME Kat was in the shower, Jonah was driving his motorcycle up to Heathrow College.

He'd been trying to get Kat off his mind all morning, but without any luck. As he walked across campus to the Natasha Pierce Building of Natural Sciences, a modern stone structure—the college's newest building, named after the deceased daughter of the town's founding family—he knew his concern for Kat was overshadowing everything, including what he'd come to Moriah's Landing to do. All morning he'd had a bad feeling that the two were somehow linked. And he always knew to trust his gut instincts.

Dr. Paul Fortier, a trim fortyish man of medium height, got up from behind his immaculately clean desk as Jonah walked in. Fortier's dark hair and beard were trimmed to perfection and his white lab coat was pristine.

Jonah didn't like him the moment he saw him. He liked him even less when he shook Fortier's weak-gripped hand, the biologist's distaste for him evident.

"What is it we can do for you, Mr. Ries?" Fortier inquired, looking down his hawkish nose at Jonah. He made it clear in his tone that he was a busy man who didn't like to have his schedule interrupted. Especially by one of the town's less desirables.

The "we" he referred to was the other biologist in his office: Dr. Rhonda Girard. A tall, thin, intense-looking blond woman, Girard also offered her hand.

Her handshake was as cool and detached as her demeanor.

Both Fortier and Girard seemed to examine him openly as if he were a bug they wished was under glass. No doubt they'd heard about his recent "release" from the FBI, which, coupled with the family name of Ries, was making them uncomfortable—and cautious.

Jonah got right to it. "I heard that some of the scientists around here are looking for guinea pigs for research projects they're doing."

"Not exactly guinea pigs," Girard said.

"Just what kind of research are we talking about?" Jonah asked.

"It's a little too complicated to explain to a layman in our current time restraints," Fortier said.

Jonah shrugged. "Genetics, right?"

Fortier gave a slight nod.

Jonah knew damn well what brought scientists like Fortier and Girard and Manning to Moriah's Landing. He'd heard rumors since he was a kid and been warned about doctors who would cage you up like a lab rat— if they got the chance—to experiment on you.

"Tell me this," he said. "What would I have to do and how much does it pay?" He saw a look pass between them. They hadn't expected this.

"You would be interested in our project?" Girard asked, obviously unable to hide her shock.

More than they could ever know. He shrugged. "It pays, right? I could use the money."

"I thought you were an agent with the FBI," Fortier asked with obvious suspicion.

"The feds and I had a falling-out," Jonah said, as if Fortier hadn't heard about it. "They felt I'd chosen the wrong career path."

He could see they were dying to get his blood, but also leery of this unexpected good fortune. It was rumored that the Ries bloodline ran back several generations, to a time when a Ries produced a son with the beautiful but wild daughter of McFarland Leary and his witch consort.

It was that kind of genetic history that had brought scientists like Fortier and Manning to Moriah's Landing in the first place. For years there'd been rumors of special powers that came with the genes of certain families—those descended from witches.

But it was also obvious that Fortier and Girard didn't want the FBI looking too closely at their research. Just paranoia when it came to the feds and how federal research funds were being spent? Or were the doctors dabbling in research they shouldn't be?

"I'm sure we can find a suitable fee if you're interested," Fortier said, obviously trying to sound as if it was no big deal—but not pulling it off. Probably because no Ries in his right mind would ever agree to any kind of genetic scrutiny. "All we would need would be a little blood. It's painless, I assure you," he added quickly as if he thought Jonah might be squeamish of needles. No, just nooses.

"Great," Jonah said.

"If you have time now," Girard said, "it will only take—"

"Sorry." Jonah feigned disappointment. "I have to get to my job and I'm running late, but let me know

when and where and how much. I'm working at the
Wharf Rat. You can reach me there.''

Fortier looked as if he wanted to grab Jonah and
open a vein with a letter opener if that's what it took
right there in the immaculate office rather than let him
get away. ''I'll call you later and set up a time.''

Jonah was sure he would.

DISTRACTED BY REMNANTS of the nightmare that had
followed her to work, Kat was startled to find another
bouquet of daisies on her office step. She knew she
shouldn't have been surprised, let alone upset at the
sight of them again, but she was. As before, they were
tied loosely with a piece of used red ribbon. She followed her first impulse and threw them in the trash
with the old ones from yesterday.

The daisies disturbed her more than she wanted to
admit. She told herself that someone was bound to
come forward to take credit for them soon. She held
on to that thought, the logic of that making her feel
better. But still, something about the daisies unnerved
her.

When she checked her messages she found one from
Bud Lawson thanking her for completing the investi-
gation so quickly. The insurance company had released
his check for repairs. Another message was from the
insurance company about Ernie McDougal's vandalism
from last night.

As with Bud Lawson, Ernie McDougal's insurance
company recommended her to investigate the damage
and turn in a report, rather than send out one of their
own agents all the way from Boston.

It was early, long before most of the shops opened, but Kat decided she'd see Ernie now and get it over with. She locked up and started down the sidewalk. Across the street, she spotted her friend Brie through the diner window and waved, feeling instantly guilty. She had only recently started socializing with Brie again. Her friend had kept to herself when Kat learned she was pregnant with her daughter, Nicole. It was as if Brie didn't want anyone to know who the father was. Kat started to cross the street to say hello to her, but Brie gave a quick wave and hurried over to a table to take an order.

Kat told herself that it was Brie who had pulled away from her friends. Brie was so busy now working at the diner, going to college and caring for her daughter and ailing mother.

"Good morning!"

Kat glanced over to find Cassandra Quintana already in her booth this morning.

"I have something for you," the fortune-teller said.

Kat would just bet she did. "Another tarot card? What is this one, death?"

Cassandra's gaze was dark and deeply intent as she shuffled the large deck of worn tarot cards in her bejeweled fingers, her bracelets tinkling. She sat at the small counter, a dark velvet cover spread before her, several candles and some incense burning on each side. "I thought you might be curious about the daisies."

Kat felt her heart take off at a run. How did Cassandra know about the daisies? "You know who left them?"

The seer shook her head, her smile sympathetic. "I only know what the cards tell me."

Right. The fortune-teller had obviously seen the person who'd been dropping off the bouquet of daisies. How else would she know about them?

Cassandra flipped a card from the deck and dropped it to the dark velvet. "I see the flowers upset you," the fortune-teller said. The whisper of another card. "I see that daisies have some significance for you, an association connected with your past that is painful. And...frightening."

Kat realized most of this the seer could have gotten from her expression alone at just the mention of the daisies. But she felt a tremor. Cassandra's words had rattled a memory awake. Daisies tied with a red ribbon. She remembered now where she'd seen the same bouquet before, the memory startling her.

Cassandra dropped another card on the velvet. "The daisies portend something that is yet to come. There is a darkness in your future. Danger."

But Kat barely heard the fortune-teller's warning. Her heart pounding, she hurried across the town green toward home. Putting down her purse, she rushed upstairs and threw open the doors to the storage area under the third-floor stairs. Frantically, she began to pull everything out, looking for the box with the old photographs her grandmother had left her.

After some frenzied digging, Kat found the box buried in the very back. Leaving everything in the middle of the hallway floor, she took the photos down to the kitchen, poured herself a strong cup of coffee, nuked it and sat down at the breakfast bar. She began going through the photos, her hands shaking.

She found what she was looking for in the middle of the box. Her fingers jerked as she unfolded the newspaper clipping. It was a front-page story about her mother's murder and consequent funeral. The photo was grainy, the faces around the grave out of focus. Instead, the camera had zoomed in on the casket and the simple bouquet of daisies tied with a worn red ribbon that someone had put on top.

Her heart beat so hard that her chest ached. She picked up one of the last photographs taken of her mother, her fingers trembling as she looked into her own face. Tears rushed her eyes, each breath a labor.

Someone was giving her the same bouquet of daisies he'd given her mother—only at her funeral.

Kat picked up her coffee cup and took a gulp, scared, but this time maybe with good reason.

"ABOUT TIME," Brody said, glancing at his watch as Jonah walked in. "You're not working for the feds now."

"Sorry," he said, glancing at his own watch. "Dock me the two minutes." He could feel Brody watching him as he stepped behind the bar, picked up the coffeepot and refilled his cousin's mug.

Brody laughed. "Maybe I will."

"With what you pay me, I'm sure I won't miss it in my check," Jonah retorted, turning away to put the coffeepot back on the burner.

Brody laughed. "No wonder the feds gave you the

boot. I've been waiting to tell you the good news. You feel lucky?''

Jonah picked up a bar rag, turned on the faucet and held the rag under it, not wanting to seem too anxious. "Not particularly."

"I got you in the game."

He turned off the faucet, wrung out the bar rag and turned slowly, frowning. "What game is that?"

"The biggest poker game in this part of Massachusetts," Brody bragged. "My poker game."

"Oh yeah?" Jonah wiped at the already clean bar. "So who plays?"

"You'll see. That is, if you have what it takes." Brody grinned. "This ain't penny-ante poker. The question is—are you man enough?"

Jonah kept scrubbing at the bar. The question had nothing to do with his manhood and they both knew it. This had to do with Ries genes. And, of course, money.

But Jonah couldn't have been happier—unless, of course, he'd never had to come back to Moriah's Landing. He wouldn't have met Kat Ridgemont though. Nor, he reminded himself, would he have known that someone was planning to kill her. However, he did not have the vaguest idea who wanted her dead or why— or how to stop it.

"Well?" Brody demanded.

"I'm always up for a friendly game of poker," Jonah said, knowing it would be anything but friendly.

Chapter Seven

The telephone rang. Kat jumped, knocking the stack of photos off the breakfast bar and spilling the last of her coffee.

Hurriedly, she mopped up the spilled coffee, shoving the photos out of the way so they didn't get wet, then reached for the phone before it could ring again.

"Hello?" She thought she heard breathing. "Hello?"

No answer. Was it one of Emily's friends, surprised to find Kat home?

She heard a soft click and shivered. Now she was letting even wrong numbers scare her, she thought, angry with her heart for pounding so hard.

She tried to walk off her bad mood by taking the long way down Main Street to Waterfront Avenue. But she couldn't forget the daisy bouquet. Or the eerie resemblance between her mother and her at this age.

Why did she feel as if she had something to fear? It wasn't as if anyone had threatened her.

As she turned onto Waterfront, she heard the throb of a motorcycle. She swung around expecting to see Jonah coming toward her. It wasn't him but still her heart raced reminding her of exactly what she had to fear.

She rushed across the street, deciding right then and there to find out more about Jonah Ries—for her own peace of mind.

With the throb of the motorcycle's motor growing behind her, she hurriedly slipped into the Bait & Tackle. The bell over the door tinkled and Ernie looked up from behind the counter at the back, seemingly surprised to see her.

"Hello," she called as she worked her way through the racks of fishing supplies to him.

Ernie was a stocky man of about sixty-five or so, with short gray hair on an obviously balding head. He wore a red cap that read Bait & Tackle in navy. The cap made his ears stick out. She'd seen Ernie around since she was a girl, but he'd hardly ever spoken to her, just hello or a nod on the street.

Now she wondered if he wasn't shy as she held out her hand. He seemed surprised, almost confused, as if he'd forgotten who she was. Or why she was here. "I'm Kat Ridgemont, the investigator your insurance company hired to file a report on the vandalism."

He shook his head as if shaking out cobwebs. "Kat, of course. You looked so much like your mother, for a moment…" He shook his head again and offered his hand. "Of course I know you." His grip was stronger than she'd expected, his arms muscular from hauling in fish, his face tanned and weathered from the sea, reminding her of her father.

"I was wondering how long it would be before my

shop was hit," he said with disgust. "Come around here and I'll show you."

He held the back door open for her, reminding her that he was from a generation of men who still believed in chivalry.

She tailed him to the side of his building to the place where she'd seen the vandals applying spray paint last night.

"I guess I'm lucky this is all they did," Ernie said.

"You're covered by insurance, but you realize repainting the wall won't exceed your deductible," she said, wondering why he'd called the insurance company for such a small claim.

"I suppose there isn't that much damage," he said thoughtfully.

She nodded, studying the seemingly hurried swaths of paint on the old brick wall. "Not exactly artistic," she commented. The vandals had taken more time on Bud Lawson's walls, but then they hadn't been interrupted as they were last night. "Any idea who might have done this?"

"Kids." Unlike Bud Lawson, Ernie didn't seem that upset.

"Have any kids been hanging around, acting suspicious?" she asked.

"Not that I've noticed. I've been getting ready for the season, so I haven't been paying much attention." Tourist season. "The usual kids hang out at the arcade down the street."

Yes, the arcade.

"I can file a report with the insurance company if

you want me to," she said, pulling out her notebook and pen.

"No, you're right. No reason to. Just drive up my rates. I should have thought of that before I called them and had them send you over. I'm sorry to have wasted your time."

She put her notebook and pen back into her purse. "No problem."

Ernie walked her back to the sidewalk in front of Bait & Tackle. He seemed to search for something to say, then settled on "Thanks."

"I've been meaning to ask you. Tommy Cavendish said he's working for you this summer."

Ernie nodded. "Running errands. Saves me having to take things down to the docks that my crews forget. Why? You don't think he was one of the vandals."

"No," she said, shaking her head. "I was just thinking about hiring him to do some things for me. He's a good worker?"

"He's okay, he's a kid," Ernie said, and shrugged, squinting at her and into the bright sun.

"I heard he's also running errands for Brody Ries."

"I wouldn't know." The phone rang inside the Bait & Tackle and Ernie excused himself to go answer it. He turned once to look back at her.

She waved and then, against her better judgment, glanced across the street to the Wharf Rat where Jonah's motorcycle was parked out front. He was nowhere in sight, thankfully.

But Kat hadn't gone two steps when Jonah fell in beside her, startling her.

"Hello," he said, his voice deep, setting a tremor off inside her. "I wanted to apologize for last night."

"What for?" she asked, pretending the kiss hadn't meant a thing to her.

"For not offering to walk you home," he said.

She stumbled and looked over at him in disbelief.

"Oh, did you think I was going to apologize for kissing you?" He smiled, sharklike. "I'm not sorry about that at all. In fact, if you give me the chance…" He laughed. "Got to get to work. Nice seeing you."

She stopped to watch him jog back to the Wharf Rat. The man was impossible. She mentally kicked herself for still being attracted to him. Like mother like daughter.

BACK AT HER OFFICE, Kat was surprised to find a message on her answering machine from Dr. Leland Manning, a local scientist who lived in town and, according to local folklore, did strange experiments in his laboratory.

"Ms. Ridgemont, if you could call me regarding an urgent personal and very private matter, I would greatly appreciate it," Manning had said in a clipped, officious tone.

She dialed the number the doctor had left, curious beyond words. She'd never even seen Manning, let alone talked to him, and now here he was asking her to call.

An older-sounding woman with a European accent answered the phone. "The doctor is unavailable. May I take a message?"

"Just tell him Kat Ridgemont of Ridgemont Detec-

tive Agency returned his call. I will be out of my office—''

''Ms. Ridgemont,'' Dr. Manning broke in, his voice
just as clipped and cool as it had been on the answering
machine. ''How good of you to call so promptly. I
would like to discuss acquiring your services.''

She blinked, caught between curiosity and uncertainty. Why would Dr. Manning possibly want to hire
her? ''I'm free this afternoon—''

''I'm afraid I'm tied up until later on in the evening,'' the doctor interrupted, ''but it is of utmost im-
portance that I speak with you in person tonight. It will
have to be late because of a previous engagement. Say,
nine-thirty? At my home?''

She'd had a mental image of the Manning estate
since she was a kid. Tall, dark spires that rose above
the gnarled trees, hidden behind an electric fence, like
some brooding entity. In her mind, it made The Bluffs,
a castle at the edge of the sea where the town's local
hermit, David Bryson, lived, look like Candyland.

And go out there after dark?

But she wasn't one to turn tail and run from anything
any more than she was apt to turn down a job without
a good reason. ''Nine-thirty is fine,'' she said, assuring
herself there was a very good explanation why no one
had ever seen Dr. Manning in the daylight. Why few
people had ever seen him at all. ''But can you tell me
what this is about?''

''I'd rather not discuss it on the phone. Until nine-
thirty then.'' He rang off.

Just before she hung up, she heard a click on the
phone as another line disconnected. She wondered if

the older woman she'd talked to first had been on the entire time. Or if it had been someone else at the estate? Hadn't she heard that Dr. Manning had married? A much younger woman. The word around town was that she never left the estate.

Kat replaced the receiver, torn between curiosity and apprehension. She didn't like the idea of going out there at night, though.

The other message on her answering machine had been from her friend Elizabeth—and was about the wedding. At least that's what Elizabeth said it was about. Elizabeth had never been a good liar. Kat hoped everything was all right.

As Jonah unlocked his door, he knew someone had been in his apartment before he even saw the tiny piece of dental floss already on the floor. Brody?

Cautiously, he opened the door. The nice thing about a studio apartment was the lack of adequate places for a man of any size to hide. He stepped into the room, moving quickly and quietly to the bathroom. No one behind the cheap plastic curtain in the shower stall. Nor anyone hiding behind the bathroom door.

He glanced around the apartment. Nothing looked out of place or gone. But maybe the intruder hadn't come to steal anything. Maybe he'd come to leave something behind—like a bug.

Stepping to the couch, Jonah reached under to the thin shelf holding his laptop. The computer was still there and it didn't appear it had been touched. He could see Brody looking under a couch cushion, maybe even bending down enough to peek under the couch, but his

cousin would never get down on his hands and knees—
and that's what it would have taken.

Jonah booted up the laptop. He ran a check on Cassandra Quintana. No big surprise. Either Cassandra
Quintana wasn't her real name or she had never bothered with a social security card or any other identifi-
cation.

"About time," flashed on in the message box.

"What's up?" he answered.

"We got another anonymous tip."

Jonah groaned. "What now?"

"Our anonymous source thinks shipment coming in
tomorrow night on *Audrey Lynn*."

Jonah jumped at the sudden loud knock on his apartment door, followed almost immediately by Brody's
strident voice.

"Open up."

The computer screen flashed. "BTW." Online lingo
for "by the way." "That name you asked about—
Ridgemont. We just picked it up on Dr. Manning's
phone surveillance. Not Leslie. Kat? Meeting him tonight, nine-thirty, his place."

"OKAY, WHAT'S REALLY bothering you?" Kat asked after she and Elizabeth were seated in her friend's living
room. "I know you too well. You didn't just invite me
here to talk about the wedding."

Elizabeth wasn't just a brain. She was refined and
beautiful with long brown hair that, until recently,
she'd worn in a bun. It seemed she'd let her hair down
since her love affair with the local cop.

Elizabeth gave her a sheepish look. Deceit was

something her friend failed at miserably. "I just thought you ought to know. There is a man in town asking questions about you and your mother."

Kat stared at her, remembering the man in the army jacket. "What man?"

"Cullen said his name is Jonah Ries."

Jonah? "What kind of questions is he asking about my mother?" She could understand Jonah asking about her. Kinda. But her mother?

Elizabeth looked uncomfortable. "Then you know him?" She sounded surprised—and worried. "Cullen says he's a former FBI agent and that there are federal charges pending against him. He sounds dangerous."

More than Elizabeth could know. "Liz, I appreciate you worrying about me—"

"Okay, butt out, right?"

"No, I just…What about my mother?"

Elizabeth seemed to hesitate. "He's been inquiring about her murder."

Kat couldn't hide her surprise. What possible interest could Jonah have in her mother's murder? She looked at her watch, wondering if she had time to stop by the Wharf Rat before she met with Dr. Manning.

"Look, I'm sorry, this has obviously upset you," Elizabeth said.

"No, I'm glad you told me. I just can't talk about this right now. I have an appointment."

"This late at night?" Elizabeth frowned. "Not with—"

"No, not with Mr. Ries. But don't worry. I can handle this." She hoped.

"I know you can." Elizabeth sounded relieved. "I

should have known you wouldn't get involved with anyone like that. I mean, not—''

"Again?" Elizabeth had found out about the abusive relationship Kat had had. Kat almost confessed to her right then and there just how scared she was about her…attraction to Jonah. Was there a twelve-step program for women like her? But she didn't want to worry her friend, not with the wedding less than two weeks away.

Kat told herself she was too smart to let another man hurt her. The problem was, she was having trouble believing that Jonah Ries was dangerous. Why was that?

Because of his kiss? Or because of the way he'd been with Tommy? She knew she could never get him off her mind until she got to the heart of the matter, so to speak. Until she found out what he was doing in Moriah's Landing and why he seemed to have taken such an interest in her—and her mother's murder.

"You must have a million things to worry about other than me," Kat said to her friend. "Getting cold feet?"

Elizabeth laughed and shook her head. "I'm busy, but I think I'm on top of it."

That was so like Elizabeth. "You look happy. Radiant, as corny as that sounds." She gave her friend a hug. "Thanks for the concern."

"If you need me—"

"I know," Kat said, but right now she just needed answers and there was only one person who had those—Jonah Ries. Unfortunately, she had just enough time to get to Dr. Manning's. Jonah would have to wait.

Chapter Eight

"Come on," Brody yelled, banging on the door again.

Jonah stared at the computer screen, that bad feeling in his gut stronger than ever. What the hell was Kat thinking, going out to Manning's alone late at night?

He clicked off, closed the computer on his way to the bathroom, stashed the laptop under some towels and called out, "Just a minute" as he flushed the toilet. "Who is it?" he asked as he neared the door.

"Who do you think?" Brody snapped.

Jonah unlocked the door, surprised Brody hadn't just used his key. "Yeah?"

"You got another shirt?" Brody pushed his way in, bringing with him a cloud of cigar smoke. Jonah noticed his cousin was dressed like a pimp in a pair of burgundy slacks, a brightly striped gold and burgundy shirt, white patent-leather shoes and enough gold to require an armored car.

Jonah looked down at the shirt he had on, his favorite wash-worn chambray one. "What's wrong with this one?"

"Put on a decent shirt if you own one," Brody snapped. "I don't want you looking like a bum."

Jonah glanced at his watch. Way too early for the poker game, unless—

"Come on, the game's been moved up." Brody peered nervously around the apartment as if looking for something. "You got any money?"

"You want to borrow some?" Jonah asked as he unbuttoned his shirt, pulled another one down from the makeshift open shelves at the end of the couch and put it on.

"Funny." His cousin started to sit down on the dilapidated couch, then changed his mind.

Jonah buttoned up the clean shirt he'd put on, avoiding Brody's gaze. "You never did say who was going to be in the game." It would be a complete waste of his time if Dr. Manning wasn't there—and after what he'd heard about Kat meeting Manning tonight at nine-thirty—

"No, I never did say."

He turned to see his cousin puffing on his cigar and eyeing him with suspicion. "Does it make a difference?"

"Just curious," Jonah said with a shrug.

Brody continued to eye him, as if worrying he might have made a mistake.

Jonah *was* surprised Brody had asked him to the poker game this soon. Something was up. Either Brody was motivated by greed—thinking Jonah would make a great mark—or he was hoping Jonah would do the fleecing. Why did he feel as if this was a test?

"Don't make me sorry I asked you," Brody said after a moment.

Jonah took the warning to heart. He'd seen Brody

almost kill a man once on the wharf. He'd been ten or eleven, which would have made Brody about nineteen, just a kid, but with a man's temper. The fisherman had been big and strong, but not as fast as Brody—or as mean. If one of the other fishermen hadn't come along and helped Jonah pull his cousin off, Brody would have killed the man.

As it was, Brody never forgave Jonah for interfering. It was just another sore point between them—and another reason Brody would never trust him completely. But blood was blood, especially in this town.

"Ready?" Brody asked, eyeing Jonah's only clean shirt. "I thought I told you this wasn't penny-ante poker." But Jonah could tell Brody was pleased that his cousin looked like the bartender he'd become. "I should have loaned you something decent to wear."

Jonah shuddered at the thought.

Once in the hallway, Brody headed to the back of the building. The smell of stale beer wafted up from the Wharf Rat below, along with the sounds of music and loud voices.

Jonah was surprised to find out the game was held in one of the larger apartments at the back, over the bar. It was quieter here and the smell of old beer not quite so strong.

"I thought this was a high-class card game," he said, needling his cousin.

"Like you'd know class if it came up and bit you in the rear," Brody retorted.

The apartment wasn't much better than the one Jonah was living in, it was just larger and the carpet was chartreuse shag instead of orange.

The kitchen had a better fridge, as it turned out, one stocked with beer, and a small bar with hard liquor and clean bar glasses. Jonah was afraid Brody might have brought him here to serve the drinks instead of play in the game, but then Brody would have to pay him.

The living room had a large octagonal poker table, complete with green felt and eight chairs. A swamp cooler pumped in cool air. That appeared to be the only furniture in the one-bedroom apartment. Through the doorway, he could see an empty bedroom and a bath with a tub but no shower curtain.

"Nice place," Jonah commented.

"It works," Brody said, obviously distracted.

Jonah saw him glance at his watch. He could tell that his cousin was nervous. Because the others didn't know that he'd invited Jonah to play? Or because of the real reason Brody had invited him? What was his cousin up to?

There was a tap at the door and Brody almost jumped out of his skin. Suddenly Jonah felt naked without a weapon snug against his ribs. But he hadn't dared wear one tonight, even if he could have hidden it under his shirt. There was too much chance that he might have been frisked.

He couldn't help worrying about why his cousin was so nervous as Brody went to the door. Dr. Leland Manning walked in—Jonah recognized him from an FBI photograph he'd been given of the man—and then he had a pretty good idea what had Brody on edge. The man was damn disconcerting.

"This is my cousin Jonah, the one I told you about,"

Brody said, obviously anxious about the scientist's re-action.

Out of the corner of his eye, Jonah watched Brody sweat while Dr. Manning gave him the once-over. Manning was a rather large but slim man in his fifties with the damnedest eyes Jonah had ever seen. Like a blowtorch, they seemed to cut to your core, boring so deep into you until you could swear the doctor knew your every thought.

Jonah waited, not wanting to appear too anxious, his mind blank, just in case the doctor really could read his mind.

Brody seemed to finally remember his manners. "This is Dr. Leland Manning, the—"

"—leading genetics-research scientist in the country," Jonah said.

"In the world," Manning corrected with a smile, his teeth small and sharp-looking. He extended his hand.

Jonah had touched fish that were warmer.

"You're interested in genetics?" Manning asked.

"As a matter of fact I am, if it can explain how Brody and I could be cousins," Jonah quipped, getting the laugh he'd hoped for.

Brody scowled at him. "A real comedian."

"Brody tells me you were in the FBI for a while," Dr. Manning said.

"For a while."

"Now you're bartending at the Wharf Rat," the doctor said. "That's quite a fall from grace."

"Yeah," Jonah admitted. "But I don't plan on being a bartender for long."

Dr. Manning nodded at that.

Brody seemed to relax, offering the doctor a drink. At the next tap at the door, he sent Jonah to get it. Jonah figured he'd passed the first test. So why did he feel there would be other, tougher tests tonight and unpleasant consequences if he failed?

Marley Glasglow filled the doorway. Jonah remembered him, a bully with a mean streak.

"Glasglow," he said with a nod, noticing the bulge under the man's jacket. It appeared at least one of them was armed. Definitely cause for concern.

Glasglow didn't respond, just pushed past him and headed for the bar. Behind him was Ernie McDougal, a quiet stocky man in his sixties.

"I don't believe we've met," Jonah said, extending his hand as he introduced himself. "Ernie McDougal, right? The Bait & Tackle?"

Ernie nodded, his hand large, his grip solid for a man his age. He didn't seem surprised to find Jonah here. Obviously, he'd already heard, just as it appeared Glasglow had.

As Jonah started to close the door, he let his gaze sweep the room. Poker brought out the best—or worst in people. Glasglow would be cutthroat and a poor loser. Manning would play for blood. McDougal? He'd play close to the vest. Brody would be as easy to read as a flashing neon sign.

"Excuse me," said a female voice through the crack in the door as Jonah was closing it.

He pulled it open again, shocked to see Cassandra Quintana standing in the doorway.

She moved past him with an annoyed shake of her head, but it wasn't until Brody offered her a drink that

Jonah believed she really was here to play poker. He groaned inwardly, wondering how many cards she had up her caftan sleeves.

Dr. Manning glanced at his watch. "You're late."

Cassandra took her drink over to a chair at the poker table, obviously her usual one. "I wasn't told there would be a guest tonight."

"He's not a guest," Brody snapped. "He's my cousin."

She raised an eyebrow, her dark gaze going from Brody to Jonah. "I still wasn't told."

"You mean, you didn't see it in the cards?" Jonah asked.

Manning actually laughed as he took his place at the table. "So tell me why you went into the FBI in the first place?"

"Damned if I know."

Manning didn't laugh this time. "What did they get you for?"

Jonah could feel the others listening with interest. "Nothing big. Falsifying records, selling documents, a little extortion." He waited until Glasglow and Mc-Dougal sat down before he took the chair farthest from the bar. It was obvious that he was the mark—and not the bartender tonight. That was Brody's job.

Brody handed him a beer as he sat down. The inquisition appearing over, Dr. Manning opened a new deck of cards, then handed them to Cassandra, who began to shuffle them like a pro—and certainly not with the reverence she used with tarot cards. More like someone who'd spent more than her share of time at a gaming table or a carny sideshow.

Jonah felt like a man in a tankful of sharks. They could smell new blood and they couldn't wait to get their teeth into him. Especially since the meat was former-FBI grade-A stock.

It proved harder to lose at poker than he'd expected. No stranger to five-card stud, he had to fight the urge to prove them wrong about him—and yet at the same time not lose so badly that it made them suspicious.

Dr. Manning played cards with an intensity that even Jonah hadn't predicted. Glasglow lost with an ugly temper tantrum. McDougal played quietly, competently and with little fanfare, just as Jonah had predicted. Cassandra played like the pro she obviously was.

"You have no business here," she said during a break in the game. He'd gone out on the fire escape for some fresh air, or at least that had been his excuse, and she'd followed him.

"You don't seem to mind taking my money," he said without looking at her. "Any way you can."

"This isn't about poker—or money," she snapped. "The stakes are higher than you think and you're in over your head."

He shrugged and turned to go back inside.

"You also aren't a very credible loser at poker," she said to his back. "You're going to get yourself killed."

Who the hell was this woman? And why did he believe her, that this wasn't about money or poker? Then what? He had a bad feeling he already knew.

They played a few more hands, with Jonah winning some small pots but losing the bigger ones to Manning. Ernie, Brody and Glasglow were all behind, Ernie losing the most. Cassandra seemed about dead even, maybe a little ahead. Manning was making a killing.

Not surprising considering that Cassandra had been tipping the doctor off on what everyone had in their hands since the first. The problem was, Jonah hadn't figured out exactly how she was doing it. Maybe the cards were marked. Or maybe she had some sort of mirror set up in this room, since she always sat in the same chair. All he knew was that she used her bracelets to signal the doctor, so it was obviously something they'd worked out.

"Are you aware that my personal research involves the descendants of witches?" Dr. Manning asked, his gaze penetrating as he swept up the cards Jonah had dealt him without looking at them.

Jonah didn't even flinch as he picked up his cards and pretended to study them. And he'd thought Brody had invited him to the game to take his money. Instead, it seemed the invite had come from Manning, and for entirely different reasons—just as Cassandra had insinuated on the fire escape. And just as Jonah had feared.

"You know witches really never did fly on brooms," Jonah said.

Manning regarded him intently. "For thousands of years, there *is* evidence to suggest, however, that they did possess psychic abilities and possibly other gifts that I believe were handed down from each generation to the next through the genes. Does that interest you?"

"Sounds more up Cassandra's alley to me," Jonah said as he pulled three cards from his hand and dropped them facedown on the table, glancing over at her.

Her gaze didn't even waver as she threw in her hand.

Brody, Ernie and Glasglow did the same, both Brody and Glasglow adding a few choice expletives.

"How many cards would you like?" Jonah asked the doctor.

"I think I'll keep the ones I have. Your lack of interest in this matter surprises me, given that your family is descended from one of the town's most famous witches, Seama," Manning said, obviously not going to let the subject drop.

"If you listen to local gossips, most everyone in town is related to Seama." Jonah smiled. "But if it were true, then I would be able to read your mind and know exactly which cards you have in your hand. Hell, I might even be able to know what the next cards in the deck are."

Jonah met Manning's gaze and saw a flicker of concern—and interest. Manning didn't want to lose this hand—or any hand for that matter. He also desperately wanted to know if Jonah possessed the gene he believed triggered these powers in families like the Rieses.

"Are you going to play poker or talk?" Ernie asked irritably.

"Mr. McDougal here has no psychic abilities at all," Manning commented. "Nor social skills."

Ernie shook his head in disgust and leaned back in his chair.

Jonah slowly drew two cards off the top of the deck, smiled and looked over at Manning before he dropped three jacks and a pair of eights to the table. "It seems the next two cards were eights."

Manning fanned his cards out on the table. Three kings and a pair of tens.

"Just my luck." Jonah got up from the table abruptly, pretending to be upset as he started to clear the table of glasses, careful not to smudge Cassandra's prints as he headed for the bar where he hid her glass until he could get it to a fingerprint lab.

"Don't go away mad," Glasglow said, sounding pleased.

"Perhaps you'd like to play one more game, try to win back what you lost?" Manning, it seemed, hadn't gotten enough blood.

"Not the way my luck is running," Jonah said.

"It will give you a chance to save face and win back some of your money," the doctor persisted.

"Or let you take my last dime," Jonah said, turning from the bar.

Manning shrugged. "It's entirely in the cards."

Yeah, right. Jonah felt Cassandra watching him, waiting, as if knowing exactly what he'd do. It made him more uneasy than he wanted to admit, because he still hadn't figured out how she was cheating. Or why she was working with Manning. Or worse, why she seemed to have taken an interest in Jonah himself.

"One more game," the doctor demanded.

No one had moved, although everyone but Manning had picked up his money for the night.

Jonah now knew why Brody had brought him here. "Sorry, but I'm a working man and I have the early shift at the bar in the morning."

Brody looked as if he might have a coronary. "Hey, I can call in another bartender for your shift—"

"If you want to always be a bartender..." Manning made a show of gathering up the money he'd won.

Jonah got himself another beer. "Oh, what the hell." He went back to the table. He could almost taste Brody's relief.

"Count me out," Ernie McDougal said. Everyone else echoed him, but didn't move. It was obvious they were all staying to see this.

"I'll take another drink," Cassandra said to Brody, settling into her chair across from Manning and to the left of Jonah.

Manning handed Jonah the cards. "You may deal."

Jonah nodded and began to shuffle, trying to decide how to make this work to his advantage. The cards were good to him and he upped the ante to everything he had on him.

True to form, Manning raised it, knowing Jonah had nothing more to bet.

"Sorry," Jonah said in defeat. "I'm busted."

Manning seemed to consider that for a moment. "Perhaps you have something to bet besides money?"

Playing dumb, Jonah looked down at the cheap watch on his arm then at Manning. The doctor shook his head. "Other than the shirt on my back—"

"Perhaps a sample of your blood," Manning suggested impatiently.

Jonah could feel the tension, tight as piano wire as they finally got down to their real reason for being here tonight. He smiled. "And if *you* lose, Doc?"

Manning's gaze bored into him. "Did you have something in mind?"

Jonah went for the one thing he knew Manning

would hate the most. "I'd like to see your lab." Manning didn't let anyone into the inner sanctum of his laboratory and, since he'd never accepted any federal funding, he'd never had to.

He saw the doctor's startled expression, the hesitation, the uncertainty. Manning shot a look at Brody. Brody looked like death warmed over. The tension in the room rose like a high-pitched squeal, high enough to break crystal, had there been any.

"I can assure you it would be of no interest to you," Manning said carefully. "It is much like any other lab."

"I hate to hear that," Jonah said. "When I was a kid I heard you had the heads of witches and warlocks floating in gallon jars."

"That sort of thing interests you?" Manning's gaze was hot enough to fry eggs.

Jonah let out a snort. "Hell, those heads could be members of my family."

Manning appeared relieved. Jonah was just a ghoul with a morbid curiosity and Manning was a doctor with a maniac need to get true Ries blood under a microscope. All Manning had to do was take the bet. After all, what were the chances he'd lose?

"All right, Mr. Ries. If you win, you may see my personal laboratory. If I win..." He smiled. A cold feral smile that lacked any trace of real humor. Like Fortier and Girard, Manning was visibly salivating at the thought of his blood.

"You know," Jonah said as if reconsidering, "I'm not sure I want to see your lab *that* bad," he added with a laugh. "You probably don't really have heads floating in jars, do you?"

"There is only one way to find out."

Jonah nodded. Unfortunately, that was true. "You're on then. How many cards?" he asked the doctor.

Manning looked across the table at Cassandra as if considering. For the first time tonight, she didn't touch her bracelets. The doctor looked down at his hand, then up at the fortune-teller. It appeared she was no longer helping him.

"Two," he snapped, throwing down the two cards he needed replaced.

Jonah dealt Manning two cards and himself three off the top of the deck, watching Cassandra. She sipped her drink, seemingly off in her own world. Manning suddenly appeared to be damn nervous.

Jonah looked at his cards although he already knew what he'd drawn. Two aces and a jack. The aces went nicely with the two aces he already had in his hand. He glanced up at Manning and smiled.

Manning's disappointment was almost palpable as Jonah dropped the four aces to the felt. Angrily, the doctor slapped his cards down on the table, facedown.

Ernie started to reach for them, no doubt anxious to see what Manning had been holding, but the doctor stopped him from showing everyone what Jonah already knew Manning had: three queens, a deuce and a four.

Manning got to his feet, signaling that the game was over. At least for tonight.

Everyone got up to leave, all apparently anxious to get out of there. Everyone except Jonah. He leaned back in his chair and finished his beer. Brody and Cassandra were having a heated conversation over by the door, with Cassandra doing most of the talking. Jonah wished he could hear what was being said, but nearby Glasglow and Ernie McDougal were loudly discussing what time to meet for a boat charter in the morning.

"When do you wish to visit my laboratory?" Dr. Manning demanded, suddenly blocking his view of the others as he came to stand beside him.

Jonah shrugged and took a drink of his beer. "I'm afraid once I see your lab, you'll destroy all my grisly illusions of it and your work."

That seemed to take some of the starch out of the doc. "You were exceptionally lucky that last hand," Manning said, pulling up the chair next to him. It was obvious that the good doctor hated losing but was also dying to know if Jonah had gotten those aces strictly through luck—or had known they were coming up in the deck.

"As you said, it's all up to the cards," Jonah said.

Manning motioned for Brody to get him a drink, interrupting the conversation with Cassandra. Glasglow and Ernie left without even a goodbye.

As she left, Cassandra shot Jonah a look as if she knew what he was up to and that he would come to no good end. He didn't need a fortune-teller to tell him that.

Brody seemed in a real nasty mood as he went behind the bar to make Manning a drink.

"You know what's wrong with your theory on descendants of witches? If you were right, Brody would have special...powers," Jonah joked, watching his cousin pour Manning a drink, all the while grumbling under his breath.

Manning followed his gaze and shook his head. "Brody's line is flawed."

Jonah couldn't agree more.

The doctor dropped his voice. "He's the bastard child of a seafaring man with a low IQ and crude tastes, not a true Ries."

It seemed Manning had done his homework.

"You, however, I suspect are the real thing," Manning said, turning his attention back to Jonah. "One of the cleanest lines I've traced. I believe you not only knew exactly what cards I had in my hand tonight but also what the next ones in the deck were. That's an amazing talent, wouldn't you say?"

"If that were true, it would be a curse," Jonah said. "Knowing everything, feeling everything. Can you imagine how that could drive a person crazy?"

"Yes," Manning said. "I believe it had that effect on both your mother—and your father."

Jonah flinched.

The doctor drained the drink Brody handed him and rose from his chair, seeming pleased with the response he'd elicited from Jonah. "Tomorrow night. Ten. I'll try not to disappoint you."

Jonah glanced at his watch: 9:15 p.m. As he watched the doctor leave, he reminded himself that Kat Ridgemont was going out to Manning's tonight. Hopefully not for a tour of the doctor's lab. Again he wondered what could possibly possess the woman to go out there this late at night.

Chapter Nine

"I know what you're trying to do," Brody accused the moment everyone else had left. His cousin still looked a little pale and upset after his talk with Cassandra, making Jonah wish more than ever that he knew what that had been about. No doubt the fact that Cassandra hadn't helped Manning during the last game. She had been doing most of the talking, it had seemed to Jonah, making him figure she had her reasons.

"You think you can buddy up to the doc and maybe get in on some of my action," Brody charged.

Jonah watched his cousin go to the bar and pour himself a stiff drink, his head down, shoulders hunched. Trouble.

"I also heard you've been asking around about a boat," Brody snapped. "And about Leslie Ridgemont's murder."

It seemed Brody had ears in a lot of places. Jonah had known it was just a matter of time before Brody got wind of what he'd been doing. "Yeah?"

"What the hell?" his cousin demanded. "I can see how you might be interested in the boat, but Leslie Ridgemont's murder?"

"I met the daughter, Kat," he said mildly. "I was just curious."

"Sure. Like you were just curious about genetics and Manning's lab?" Brody swore. "What the hell do you think you're doing?"

He shrugged. "Just checking out all my options."

"Listen to me. You have no idea what you're getting into or who you're messing with." Brody acted scared. Certainly not for Jonah's well-being, that was for sure.

"Maybe you should tell me just what it is you think I'm messing with," Jonah suggested as he moved to the bar.

Brody took a sip of his drink, then set it down carefully on the bar. In one swift motion, he grabbed Jonah's shirt collar and jerked him partway over the small, makeshift bar. Jonah had seen it coming. Just as he could have stopped the attack, had he wanted to.

"Listen to me, you little bloodsucker," Brody spat in his face. "If it turns out that you're still working for the FBI—"

"If I was still working for the feds, I would have already busted your ass for bringing in illegal booze by boat once a month from Canada," Jonah whispered, having found the shipment last night on a boat out of New Brunswick—just not the boat he'd been looking for.

Brody blanched and let go of his collar. "How did you—"

"Don't worry about it," Jonah said. "If I wanted a piece of the action, I'd have already asked." He smiled at his cousin. "I have bigger fish to fry."

Brody swore. "What you're going to do is find yourself swimming with the fish."

Jonah laughed and straightened his shirt. "I think you underestimate me."

"That's what I'm afraid of," Brody said seriously. "You've even got Dr. Fortier at the college calling the bar, thinking you're going to give your blood to science."

Jonah shrugged. "Like I said, I'm exploring all of my options." Except Fortier had been a dead end. The doctor hadn't come up with enough money when Jonah had offered his blood—certainly not near enough to suggest anything illegal going on at the university.

"Watch yourself with Manning. He'll chew you up and spit you out," Brody warned. "Trust me, you don't want to get on that guy's wrong side."

"Is that why you let him and Cassandra cheat?" Jonah asked.

Brody blanched stark white. He opened his mouth to say something, then closed it, like a fish out of water.

"Come on, Brody, why else would you let a *woman* in your game, let alone someone as flaky as that one?" Jonah had seen the way Cassandra was talking to Brody before she left. It was so unlike Brody to take that kind of abuse from anyone—let alone a woman. Cassandra and Brody. Jonah couldn't imagine a more anomalous pair.

Brody took a moment to compose himself. Either he was surprised that Jonah was aware of the cheating or he really hadn't known. Either way, he was upset and trying damn hard not to show it. "Don't let her getup fool you. That is one sharp woman. She plays cards better than most men I've known. Just not better than Manning. Neither of them would have to cheat."

"Maybe they don't have to, but they do. She and Manning have a system where she tells him what everyone has by touching a different color bracelet."

Brody stared at him. "Bull. Do you think I wouldn't know if someone was cheating in my own card game?"

Jonah shrugged.

Brody was visibly rattled. "Yeah, well, while you're considering your options, here's one you'd better reconsider. Stay away from Kat Ridgemont."

Jonah raised an eyebrow at him. "You aren't serious? Have you seen the woman?"

"She's fine," Brody agreed. "But being around her will definitely be dangerous to your health. Take my word for it."

Jonah felt his heart begin to pound. "How could hanging around her be dangerous?"

Brody shook his head, finished his drink and went to the door. "Just consider yourself warned." He waited there for Jonah to follow him so he could lock up. Jonah would have to come back for Cassandra's glass later tonight. Getting in with these cheap locks would be a piece of cake.

"So tell me," Jonah said conversationally as they walked down the hall together, "what was Leslie Ridgemont like? I heard she was a *wild* woman."

Brody laughed and seemed to relax a little. "She was hell on wheels. She flirted with everyone who came into the diner—no matter how young or how old." He smiled over at Jonah. "She taught me everything I know."

Jonah didn't know whether to believe Brody or not. "Like hell. She wouldn't take on a punk kid like you. Shoot, you couldn't have been more than what? Fifteen? When she died?"

Brody swore. "I was seventeen and big for my age." He grinned as if in memory. "She *liked* me. Said I made her laugh."

"You're making *me* laugh," Jonah said. "She must not have been very choosy."

Brody stopped walking. He was so damn easy to get going. "I'll have you know there were a hell of a lot of guys she flirted with, but most she wouldn't even give the time of day to after working hours."

"Yeah? Name just one."

"Like...Marley Glasglow. She flirted with him all the time, had him practically crawling, and then she'd act like she didn't even know who he was when she left the diner." Brody started walking again. "Why do you think he hates women so much?"

Marley Glasglow. He'd been fifteen the spring Leslie Ridgemont was murdered—and on the town green that night.

"You don't think Marley could have killed her?" Jonah asked ghoulishly. "You were there that night, right? You must have seen him."

Brody stiffened. "I thought I told you to forget about all that. Especially the daughter. You're going to get yourself killed if you don't." He pushed open the exit and started to take the stairs down into the darkness. "Oh, one more thing. I have an errand I need you to run for me tonight."

As Jonah watched Brody go a few minutes later, he

realized his hands were shaking. Brody knew about the danger around Kat. Why was that? Hearing Brody warn him off only made it more real. And more vital that he warn Kat. If only he knew who the hell he was warning her about.

IT WAS AFTER nine-thirty when the headlights of Kat's car illuminated the sign up to the Manning estate: Private Road. No Trespassing. She turned down the narrow paved lane that cut a thin swath through the woods. Not even a glimmer of a moon or stars shone through the branches as the road wound its way up the hillside.

The isolated, tree-choked mansion had always creeped her out. Gnarled and misshapen by the wind and weather, the trees seemed to stand guard around the massive house, as protective as trolls under a bridge, as malformed as Frankenstein's monster.

She knew that wasn't all that was creeping her out. She'd made a call on her cell phone as she left Elizabeth's to her source inside the FBI. What she'd heard about Jonah Ries was true. He had been ousted from the FBI and was still facing criminal charges. What was a man like that doing asking questions about her—and her mother's murder?

Her attention was drawn back to business as the twisted road straightened, the trees drawing back a little for Dr. Manning's old mansion. A ten-foot-tall electric fence encircled it.

She stopped at the hulking gate but didn't even have time to press the intercom button before the gate swung open as if by magic. With more than her share of qualms, she drove through.

She'd heard stories about Dr. Leland Manning since she was a girl. Along with the silly rumors that he was a vampire and got his blood from the fresh corpses he used for his research were tales of a secret society of mad scientists who did Frankenstein-like experiments in their laboratories around Moriah's Landing. Dr. Manning, it was said, was the ringleader.

Kat discounted rumors. But she realized as she parked in front of the haunted-looking house, this isolated place would be the perfect hideaway for a vampire. Or a leading mad scientist.

As she opened her car door, she was struck by the quiet. In the woods around Moriah's Landing, the spring night had been alive with the reassuring sound of insects and birds. Here, she heard nothing in the impenetrable stillness. Not even a hint of a breeze. The leaves on the trees hung lifeless. Not a breath of air stirred the spring night. No scent of the sea. No whisper of life. Just one small light burning inside the house.

With her purse clutched next to her body—the Beretta and her cell phone tucked inside should she need either—she climbed out of her car. She was almost to the massive wooden door at the front of the structure when, like the gate, it swung open, startling her. She stared at an aging woman in a bad dress.

"Ms. Ridgemont," the woman said, her voice deep, her accent old-world European. "The doctor will see you in his study." The woman didn't wait, just turned on one of her blocky heels and started down a long dark hallway.

Kat followed, surprised at the furnishings. She'd expected the inside to match the outside: dated furniture, thick musty drapes, foot-worn Oriental rugs, walls gloomy and dark with aging wood.

It appeared Manning had gutted the house, then painted the interior a laboratory sterile white, filling it with chrome and sleek black modern furniture, all in stark contrast to the Munsters look of the outside.

The matron had stopped a few feet ahead of her in front of an open doorway. "Dr. Manning," she announced from the doorway. "Ms. Ridgemont."

"That will be all, Odette," said a clipped, gruff male voice.

Odette gave a slight bow then retreated to the back of the house. Kat stepped forward to peer into the study, relieved and surprised to find Dr. Manning in neither a long white lab coat or an all-black suit. An average-looking man in his fifties, the doctor stood before the small blaze burning in the marble fireplace wearing jeans, clogs and an Oxford button-down checked shirt.

Relieved, Kat stepped into the room.

Dr. Manning turned slowly. "Ms. Ridgemont."

Her relief was short-lived as she was struck by the intensity of his piercing dark gaze—and the stark whiteness of his skin.

He extended his hand. "Thank you so much for coming."

His touch startled her more than even his eyes. His hand could have been the flesh of a corpse it was so clammy and cold. He smiled as he enveloped her hand in his, giving her the impression it wasn't the first time he'd seen that reaction to his touch.

"You said on the phone that you wanted to hire

me,'' she said, hoping to get this over with as quickly as possible.

He nodded, seeming amused. "Please have a seat."

She sat on the edge of the leather couch. It, too, felt cold and damp. He took a chair across from her, crossing his legs, fastidiously adjusting one pant leg before looking at her again.

"My laboratory was broken into last night," he said. "I'm convinced the perpetrators were youths who didn't realize that they were destroying important research materials." He took a breath as if winded. "Unfortunately, what they took I must have back."

"You've contacted the police?"

He shook his head. "Let me be frank with you, Ms. Ridgemont. I'm not fond of the police. I was once young and…adventurous myself."

She couldn't imagine this man ever being either.

"I feel calling the police in on what was obviously just a prank would do these juveniles a disservice," he continued. "I don't wish for them to go to jail or to be punished. I'm sure by now they regret what they did."

She wouldn't count on that, she thought as she pulled out her notebook and pen.

"I just want my property returned," he continued. "I believe you can use discretion in finding these youths for me and making them an offer."

She looked up, startled. "An offer?"

He nodded solemnly. "I want you to offer them a reward for the return of my property, no questions asked. Does that make you uncomfortable?"

She would never be comfortable around this man,

especially with him reading her so easily. "You're talking about rewarding criminal behavior."

"I'm talking about the expedient return of my property," he corrected. "It provides me with no benefit to have these young people arrested. I don't have the time or any interest in a trial. I don't have that thirst for justice that you have. To me it's just an unfortunate incident I hope to rectify with your help."

Pen poised, she asked, "What exactly was stolen?"

"I prefer to keep that just between myself and the three young people who broke into my laboratory," he said, making her look up again in surprise.

"You saw them?" How else would he know that there were three, let alone that they were young? Her heart pounded at the thought of Emily being one of them. Is that why the doctor had "hired" her for this job? Because he knew that her half sister was involved?

Dr. Manning rose. "If you would so kindly come with me." He started out of the room and she followed, amazed that the room felt cold and drafty even with a fire going this late in May. But then the whole house felt as cold and impersonal as a morgue, she thought with a shiver.

She trailed him down the hallway to the back of the house, where he picked up a flashlight. As he opened the outside door for her, she spotted another structure hidden behind the house and surrounded by yet another substantial electrified fence. His laboratory?

She slowed her steps at the thought of actually going inside. As it turned out, she had nothing to fear. He didn't head for the locked gate, but followed the fence around to the side where she could see a few broken limbs on the ground.

"They climbed the tree and dropped to the other side of the fence, then broke in through the heating vent on the roof of the laboratory," Dr. Manning explained.

"This doesn't sound like kids," she had to tell him.

"You will see that the ground was muddy from the fog," he said, shining the beam of the flashlight under the thick branches of the tree nearest the fence.

Kat followed the beam of light, agreeing with Dr. Manning's assessment of how the thieves had gotten in based on the footprints under the tree.

The doctor reached into his pocket and withdrew what appeared to be a garage-door opener, startling her for an instant into thinking it was a stun gun. He pressed a button and a large yellow yard light flashed on, blinding her.

As she turned away from the sudden brightness, she caught movement in the shadows at the rear of the house. A young spry female in a dress sneaked along the side of the house to disappear into the darkness. Definitely not Odette, the housekeeper.

"You will note the sizes of the prints," Dr. Manning was saying, his back to the house, making her pretty sure he hadn't seen the woman. "I would say two older boys and possibly a younger boy—or a girl."

Kat bent down to inspect the impressions in the once-muddy soil in the beam of the doctor's flashlight. Three pairs of sneakers, two about size tens, she'd guess, the smaller print only slightly larger than her own size seven.

The soles of the larger two prints had left a design

in the mud. Both a popular brand of athletic shoes worn by teens. The smaller tracks had a distinct tread, but no telltale designer's name left imprinted in the mud.

Kat rose, thinking about Emily's size eight cross trainers, and at the same time wondering about the woman she'd just seen watching them from the shadows of the house, wondering what size shoe she wore.

"It must get lonely out here," she said, glancing back at the house, seeing nothing in the shadows now.

"Lonely?" He sounded as if he'd never heard the word before. "I have my work," he said in that clipped, cold tone. "I have Odette. I have my wife."

In that order?

He started back toward the house.

"Is it possible that one of them might have been responsible for any of the prints near the tree?" she had to ask.

He stopped so abruptly, she almost ran into him. "Neither Odette nor my wife wear sneakers. Those were sneaker tracks, were they not? The kind young people wear these days?"

He must get MTV in his eerie house, she thought glibly.

She nodded, looking for answers other than the obvious ones and unwilling to dismiss the woman she'd seen. If he didn't know she sneaked around at night watching him, maybe he also didn't know she wore athletic shoes when it suited her—or had reason to break into his lab in the middle of the night.

"Also Odette wears a larger shoe size than those, and my wife takes a much smaller size," Manning was saying, reading her thoughts again. "You are most welcome to inspect their feet if you don't believe me. But then why would I go to the trouble of hiring you if I thought the theft was, as they say, an inside job?''

He had a point. Also she didn't care to inspect Odette's feet, although she wouldn't have minded meeting the woman who appeared to be the doctor's much younger wife, if out of nothing more than curiosity.

"What concerns me is how the thieves were able to steal your property and yet get back over both fences with the security you have here," she told him.

"Once inside the laboratory, they shut down the power to the fences and cut exit holes with the bolt cutters I keep in there."

She didn't even want to contemplate why he kept bolt cutters in his lab. "Can I see the holes they—"

"I repaired them at once for obvious security reasons."

Was he telling her the truth?

"I have no reason to lie to you," he said, reading her perfectly—and shaking her to the soles of her own shoes. He turned and headed back toward the house.

She followed silently, disturbed by this man and confounded by why anyone would break into his lab. What had the trio taken? Something large enough they hadn't been able to climb over a fence with it.

Kat followed him back to his study, determined to pass on the case. Without a word, he pulled out a thick black checkbook from his desk drawer, opened it and picked up his pen.

"Dr. Manning—"

"I'm sure you are busy with other cases, but if you

can see your way clear to move this one to the top of your list—'' he looked up ''—I will compensate you liberally. Say, double your usual hourly rate and a generous bonus if you are successful?''

''Do you know what my usual hourly fee is?'' she asked, unnerved that he just might.

He smiled. ''It really doesn't matter.''

She watched him write something on the notepad by his phone, telling herself that money or no money she was walking away from this one. But she couldn't walk away from the fact that the girl she'd seen in a red jacket running away from the freshly spray-painted bait-shop wall might be Emily. Just as the sneaker prints near Dr. Manning's lab might be hers.

Dr. Manning slid the notepad across the desk without even looking at her.

''That is most generous,'' she said, shocked at the amount. She pulled one of her contracts from her purse before she could change her mind. So the guy was creepy. A lot of her clients were weird. It was the nature of the private-eye business.

He handed her a check for a full day's work at the ridiculously high hourly wage he'd written on the pad, then he handed her the contract he'd filled in and signed in tight, neat handwriting. She noted he'd added the part about the bonus and had written in a figure— enough money to pay almost a semester of Emily's tuition at an Ivy League college.

She put both the check and the contract in her purse next to her Beretta, feeling as if she'd just made a deal with the devil.

''I'll be anxiously waiting to hear from you,'' the

doctor said, closing the checkbook with a snap. An instant later, Odette appeared at the door to walk Kat out.

It wasn't until she was in her car, the engine running, that Kat let herself glance back at the house. A curtain flicked aside in one of the backlit second-story windows. For just an instant, a young woman's face peered out. Then the curtain dropped back into place, the room suddenly dark again. Manning's wife?

Kat hit the gas and drove toward the gate, convinced she could feel Dr. Manning's piercing eyes boring into her the whole way. He'd read her so easily, how could he not know her suspicions about Emily's involvement?

The gate swung open and she drove through without looking to see if it closed behind her. As she rounded the first corner and dropped down the hillside along the tree-lined narrow road, she looked back to see the house disappear from view. But she couldn't get rid of the uneasy feeling trailing her.

In the blackness of the trees, the car's headlights illuminated only a short stretch of road in front of her. She felt anxious. Anxious to get home and talk to Emily. Anxious to put Manning and his laboratory far behind her.

The road took a tight turn to the left, spiraling down to another tight turn to the right. She glanced at her speed, surprised how fast she was going. The steering wheel felt stiff as she made the first turn. Ahead, the single-lane road took a sharp turn to the left through the dense trees.

She let her foot up off the gas pedal, but the car sped

faster, the engine revving loudly. At the same time, she saw something ahead that made her heart stop. A light. It flickered through the branches. Someone was coming up the road toward her.

Panicked, she hit the brakes, but the pedal went to the floor. She pumped it. No brakes. She took the next turn, tires squealing on the dark pavement, the steering so hard she had to crank the wheel to keep the car on the road.

Madly, she stomped on the gas pedal, trying to get it unstuck, her panic heightening. The dense trees rushed by in a twisted murky blur, the sound of the engine roaring in her ears as she pumped again at the unresponsive brakes.

Frantic, she attempted to downshift but she was going too fast. She tried to get the car into neutral, but it wouldn't go. In final desperation, she reached for the key to kill the engine—and the emergency brake, knowing even as she grabbed for it that it probably might not work. In that instant, a motorcycle came roaring around the curve, directly into her path.

Chapter Ten

Jonah let go of the breath he'd been holding as the car skidded to a halt, only a fraction of an inch from where his motorcycle stopped.

He pushed his bike aside and up on the kickstand, then stepped around the side of the car, his legs weak, his heart a thunder in his chest. Kat's dark blue eyes were wide, one hand gripping the steering wheel, the other the handbrake.

He opened the door and leaned across her to pry her clammy fingers from the emergency brake. As he did, his body made contact with hers and he felt her jerk as if hit with a jolt of electricity. He could feel her trembling with the aftershock.

"I almost hit you," she whispered.

He nodded, well aware of that. "But you didn't," he said gently as he pulled her from behind the wheel.

Her eyes welled up and she began to shake in earnest as if she only then let herself admit how close a call it had been for both of them.

She had no idea. If he hadn't been there... He shoved the thought away as she stumbled against him. He put his arms around her as if it were the most natural thing in the world. For any other woman and man, it might have been.

But for him, her touch was pleasure and pain. She electrified his senses, blinding him with feeling and at the same time frightening him with the intensity of the danger he felt around her.

"What were you doing out here this late anyway?" he demanded, angry with her for letting herself get caught in this situation, even more angry with himself.

"My job. You might recall that I'm a private investigator."

It wasn't something he was likely to forget. "You're working on a case involving Dr. Manning?"

"Excuse me, but that's none of your business." As quickly as she'd stumbled into his arms, she was out of them. She pushed away, wiping at her eyes with still-trembling fingers, her face illuminated by the glow from the car's headlights, her expression one of anger—and suspicion. "Were you *following* me?"

He motioned to his motorcycle. "I was on my way up the road when I saw lights through the trees and heard an engine revving and tires squealing."

"So why didn't you get out of the way then?" she demanded.

"There wasn't time." It had been a fool thing to do, staying in the middle of the road like that, but he'd thought he could stop her by his strength of will if nothing else. "Had you noticed any trouble with your brakes earlier tonight?"

She blinked and looked at him. "How did you know I didn't have any brakes?" She'd gone straight from suspicion to accusation.

"I can smell the brake fluid from here and I could

see you were having trouble stopping.'' He stepped around her to reach inside the car and pull the release on the hood.

"You just happened to be coming up the road this late at night?'' She followed him around to the hood, looking a little scared and a whole lot suspicious.

"Not that it's any of your business,'' he said, mimicking her, "but I was doing my job. My boss had me bring a package up to Manning tonight.'' He motioned to the box of expensive scotch bungie-corded to the back of his bike.

She looked in that direction, her face threatening to crumble as if the fear had come back. "You could have been killed,'' she whispered.

"But I wasn't and, fortunately, neither were you,'' he said softly, touching her arm.

She nodded, fighting back tears, and hugged herself as she looked away.

He pulled the small high-powered flashlight he carried from his jacket pocket and shone the beam onto the engine, not surprised to find the throttle wired so once it was started it would stay open. With his shirttail he removed the hot wire and slipped it into his jacket pocket.

"Well?'' she said, turning around to look under the hood with him.

He stared down at the engine for a moment. "Afraid I don't know much about car engines...''

She groaned and slammed the hood, barely missing his head. "A lot of help you are. Probably just a sticky throttle. Maybe the brakes got wet.''

He could see she was searching for an answer other than the obvious one. He moved around to the side, tugged off his leather jacket and laid it over the top of her car before he slithered under to check the brakes. He found the brake line had been cut. No big surprise.

"Did you see anyone else on the road or near Manning's house?" he asked as he slid out and got to his feet again, shrugging back into his jacket.

Her eyes narrowed. "Why?"

"Someone cut your brake line," he said matter-of-factly.

"It must have cracked. Or maybe a rock cut it." She was shaking her head as she squatted down to look under the car. It was obvious that she didn't know anything about cars.

"Believe me, it was cut. And by a knife—not a rock."

"Why would anyone do that and why would I believe you?"

He had a real good idea why someone had done it, but not one he could share with her. "I would imagine in your profession you might have made a few enemies," he suggested, pulling the wire from his pocket. He hadn't wanted to scare her, but now he realized he could use it to his advantage. "This was holding your throttle open."

Her gaze came up to meet his. For just an instant, she questioned whether someone could have deliberately tried to injure her. The idea obviously shocked her. She instantly rejected it with a laugh. "Not with the kind of cases I take."

He wasn't so sure about that. But it wasn't one of her cases that was the problem here.

"Trust me, there'll be a good explanation for what

happened tonight,'' she said. ''And who knows where you got that wire.''

There was a good explanation, but he didn't think she would believe that, either. He looked into her eyes, worried that he might blow the progress he'd made if he wasn't careful, but desperately needing to be totally honest with her.

''Look, you're in danger.''

''If this is about my brake line being cut—''

''Someone is trying to kill you.''

She raised an eyebrow. ''You got all that from a near-accident?''

''Let me explain. It's about this little family quirk—''

''Mine or yours?'' she asked.

''Mine.''

''I know what the town says about your family. But I know your family isn't really descended from Mc-Farland Leary and his supposed witch consort,'' she said. ''Not that it would make any difference. They were just people. Everyone knows all of that burning at the stake and hanging of witches was just hysteria on the part of ignorant people.''

He winced as if he'd been at the hanging.

Her look turned tender. ''Even if you are related to them, it wouldn't make you…odd or different from anyone else unless you believed that you were. Which you're not. I mean, I can tell that.''

He opened his mouth to speak, closed it again and said, ''That's very understanding of you.''

''I know what it is like to have people talking about your family,'' she continued. ''I'm sure you've heard about my mother. Everyone has.''

He thought about playing dumb, but didn't want to with her. "She liked men. That isn't a crime."

"No, but if she'd been faithful to my father while he was at sea, maybe she'd still be alive."

That would depend on who killed her. But he didn't tell her that. "Look, someone cut your brake line and rigged the throttle," he said, trying to get her back to the subject. "I think we should call the police and have them—"

"Not until I have a qualified mechanic look at the damage," she said. "After all, I did stop, didn't I?"

She had him there. He couldn't tell her *how* she'd stopped. She wouldn't believe him if he did. Forget total honesty.

"I think you're overreacting." She started to move past him as if she thought she was going somewhere in that car.

He didn't think so. He pulled his cell phone from his leather jacket and punched in the number of the local garage, asked for a tow truck, gave their location and hung up.

She was staring at him. "A cell phone?" she demanded.

Obviously, she didn't see him as being a cell phone kind of guy. "It's a friend's."

"I can call my own tow truck," she said, sounding put out.

"Sorry, I was just trying to help."

"What you don't seem to get is that I'm not a helpless female. I can take care of myself."

Under normal circumstances, he didn't doubt that for a minute. But Kat didn't have the faintest idea what was after her. Neither did he for that matter.

"So if you don't mind, Mr. Ries—"

"Jonah." He crossed his arms and leaned against her car to wait for the tow truck.

She studied him for a moment. "Isn't there someplace you're supposed to be?" she asked, motioning to the booze on the back of his bike. It was obvious that she felt safer alone out here than with him. Under normal circumstances, she would be right.

"The scotch will just be a little older when I get it there," he said.

She planted her hands on her hips. Very nice hips, too. And let out a long sigh as she leaned against the car and looked up at the dark night sky. She looked so damn sexy with her head thrown back like that.

He could feel the fog moving in off the ocean and hear the tow truck already coming up the hill. The towing service was just at the end of town, and Doug, the owner, lived upstairs over the garage, so Jonah had known it wouldn't take long. "I could give you a ride back into town."

"Does hard of hearing run in your family? Is that the 'quirk' you were going to tell me about?"

He smiled and shook his head.

"Then goodbye, Mr. Ries. I'll catch a ride with the tow truck."

He didn't need her to hit him over the head. But still he waited until the truck lumbered to a stop and a harmless enough looking young man in his late teens climbed out of the cab.

Jonah hung around until the kid got the car hooked on and Kat was seated in the truck cab. Getting on his motorcycle, Jonah duck-walked it over to the passenger side of the tow truck. He waited until Kat rolled down her window. "See you around."

"Not if I see you first," she said as she rolled up the window. He smiled in spite of himself as he started his bike and roared off up the road toward the doc's place to deliver the case of scotch Brody had insisted he bring out tonight.

Once away from Kat and assured she was safe for the moment, he let himself feel the anger and the fear. He'd been set up tonight. Someone had wanted to know more about the Ries genes and had almost gotten Kat killed in the process. Brody? Dr. Manning? Either way, he planned to find out and make sure they never pulled a stunt like that again.

KAT LEFT HER CAR at the garage to be fixed, went home and changed into jeans and a crop top, hoping not to look so conspicuous as she entered the arcade. She just wanted to get this job for Dr. Manning over with. It wasn't quite eleven but she was surprised to find so many kids still out even with school getting out, in a matter of days.

She wandered through the kids hunched over the noisy machines, looking for Dodie and Razz. Even if they hadn't broken into Dr. Manning's lab, they'd probably know who had or could find out a lot easier than she could. She also had a feeling that the allure of easy cash would appeal to the two.

Later she would deal with finding out whether or not her little sister might be involved. Just the thought left her sick with worry.

She spotted Razz at a game called Assassin Station zapping creatures of all kinds with what appeared to be an AK-47. Great game for a guy like him. Razz was the same age as Kat, but he dressed as if he was still in high school and hung out with Dodie, who was around Emily's age. Both Razz and Dodie had dropped out of high school and didn't seem to have a life plan other than bullying the younger kids, hanging out at the arcade and getting into trouble.

Razz wore torn and tattered jeans, a gimme T-shirt from a local lube shop and a gimme Bait & Tackle cap from Ernie's, the cap dark with filth and on backward. He was so engrossed in his game, he didn't even hear her approach until she leaned over to obscure his next shot.

"What the hell?" he demanded, finally seeing her.

"I need to talk to you," she said, still blocking his view of the game.

"Well, it can wait until I finish this game."

"I don't think so," she said. "Let's go outside."

Razz swore and, for a moment, looked as though he wouldn't cooperate.

"Dr. Manning sent me," she said.

His expression gave him away. She saw him look around for Dodie. But the younger punk was nowhere to be seen.

Resigned, Razz went outside with her, nervously glancing over his shoulder, obviously not as sure of himself without Dodie. "So what do you want?"

"Dr. Manning's laboratory was broken into last night. He wants what was taken, no questions asked. He's willing to pay for its return, if it's tonight." Kat added the time constraint as an incentive.

Razz looked worried. "What does that have to do with me?"

She gave him her best duh-look.

"I don't know anything about it," he said, feigning hurt as he adjusted his cap.

"Whatever." She started to turn and leave.

"Hey, I might know who did though."

She stopped and turned back to him. He belonged in jail—not rewarded for his theft, but this was Manning's call. "Who might?"

He gave her *his* best duh-look.

Resigned, she said, "Dr. Manning will pay a sizable reward for the merchandise's return. He'd like it back by midnight."

Razz ran a tongue over his dry lips. "How sizable?"

She shook her head, but she could see Razz's interest had been piqued. Curiosity and greed were such great motivators. She watched him glance at his watch, real nervous now. It was after eleven.

"One more thing," she said. "Dr. Manning found tracks on the ground the night of the break-in and knows that there were three trespassers. Based on shoe sizes, it looks as if one of the three was a girl." Kat watched his face, her heart pounding. "I want the name of that girl."

"Even if I knew…" He let out a groan. "Oh, I get it. You think maybe your kid sister was one of them?" He seemed to find that amusing.

"Was she?"

"How would I know?"

She was tempted to wipe the arrogance from his face.

He stepped back as if he feared she just might try.

"I'll ask around," he said, and disappeared back into the arcade.

But not before she noticed the brand name of the athletic shoes he had on—and estimated the size. Not surprisingly, they could have been a match for one of the sets of prints under the tree on Dr. Manning's property.

Kat started home, fairly sure Dr. Manning would have his property back by midnight. If only she could be sure that Emily hadn't been the girl vandal.

Once she left Main Street, she found the streets dark and deserted. Wisps of fog moved up from the cove on a sea breeze that smelled of fish and brine. As she started along the brick path through the park and town green, Kat heard footsteps echoing behind her.

She turned, seeing no one. Clouds moved restlessly across the moon, casting odd shadows over the town green. The fog moved along the ground, curling around the trunks of the trees, obscuring the ground. If someone really was following her, he must have stepped off the path behind one of the many trees.

She picked up her pace, the echo of the footfalls behind her, but each time she turned, she would see nothing or only catch what might have been a glimpse of movement near the trees. She couldn't help but think about what Jonah had said to her about being in danger. She'd thought he was just trying to scare her. She was almost running by the time she reached the house, relieved to see lights on inside.

"Hey!" her sister said as Kat locked the front door behind her and tried to calm down. Glancing out the window, she saw no one, but she wasn't fool enough to think someone hadn't been out there or that she hadn't been followed home. Again.

Emily had a plate filled with nachos and was headed

for her room, where the volume of music coming out of the stereo was rattling the windows. "Where's your car?" Em yelled over the noise.

"Had some trouble with the brakes," Kat yelled back, still a little shaken from her close call and now wondering if the brake line really had been cut, the throttle not just stuck but wired open. But why? It made no sense. "Could you turn that down and then come into the living room. I need to talk to you."

Emily's expression closed. "What now?" she asked with a groan.

Kat motioned for her to turn down the stereo first. "I just need to talk to you."

"Yeah, right." Em set down her nachos on the table by the door next to the phone and climbed the stairs to turn down the music as if she were headed for a hanging.

Kat checked the answering machine. No messages. No big surprise. But she had expected Ross to call even though she hadn't planned to see him again. Maybe Elizabeth was right. Maybe she did intimidate men. Except for men like Jonah, she thought with a silent groan.

Kat took a chair in the living room, a room filled with furniture that had been in the family for years, a mixture of styles and colors, but too homey to even consider replacing if she were so inclined—which she wasn't.

She looked up as the noise stopped and Emily slinked back down the steps, picked up her nachos and plopped sullenly into a chair across from her. "Okay, what have I done now?"

"I need to ask you about something I saw earlier," Kat said, not sure how to broach the subject, but she noticed her sister suddenly seemed nervous. She didn't want to accuse Emily of vandalism and she sure as the devil didn't want to believe that Em had had anything to do with breaking into Dr. Manning's lab, but she also couldn't ignore what she'd seen—a young female vandal wearing a jacket exactly like Em's running from the scene.

"Where's the red jacket I bought you?" she asked, glancing toward the coatrack by the door, already aware that it wasn't hanging there.

Em rolled her eyes and made an impatient groan. "You want to talk about my *jacket?*"

"Where is it?" Kat asked again, not about to be dissuaded.

"I don't know," Emily snapped. "Probably around somewhere."

"Would you mind finding it for me?"

"You *aren't* serious?"

Kat just gave her a look and waited. Emily uncurled herself from the chair, her plate of nachos slamming down a little too hard on the coffee table as she stomped up the stairs again. Kat could hear her rummaging around in her room, swearing. She wished she didn't have to have this relationship with her sister. But without parents to guide Em, Kat found herself in that role.

She turned at the sound of Em's bare feet thumping down the stairs again. "I can't find it, all right?"

"Do you remember the last time you wore it?" Kat persisted.

Em rolled her eyes and dropped into the chair again. She pulled the plate of nachos onto her lap and resumed eating, obviously angry. "This morning, I guess. Maybe I left it at school."

Kat knew the signs of lying: avoiding eye contact, rubbing the nose, putting too much interest in something uninteresting like the melted cheese on a nacho chip. Em was lying about the jacket and Kat could only think of one reason why.

"I saw some kids spray painting the side of the Bait & Tackle last night. One of them was wearing a red jacket."

Em's head snapped up, her eyes widening. "You think I was one of them?" she demanded, sounding both insulted and surprised.

"Were you?"

Em opened her mouth and shook her head as if at a loss for words. "You're accusing *me!*" Emily was on her feet, the nachos flying. "I can't believe this."

"Yes or no?" Kat asked.

"No!" Emily's glare dared her not to believe it.

Kat realized she hadn't been keeping close enough tabs on her half sister. She didn't know what kids she hung out with or where she went or what she did lately. "Then you can tell me where you were yesterday and who you were with?"

Em's face instantly closed. "I was with some friends."

"Who?" Kat asked, feeling like a warden instead of a sister.

"Just a bunch of kids," Emily snapped, looking close to tears and at the same time angry. "I'm almost eighteen!" She said it as if it were a threat. Then she sighed. "Okay, I wasn't with anyone. I had a fight with Angela." Angela was her best friend and a girl that

Kat worried wasn't a good influence on Em. "I just took off walking by myself, but I don't expect you to believe that."

Kat wished she could, but Em wouldn't look her in the eye and seemed nervous. "Someone also broke into Dr. Manning's lab last night and stole his property," she said, watching her sister's face, afraid of the re-action she was going to get. "We're not talking about a prank. We're talking about breaking and entering and burglary, a punishable crime."

"Someone broke into Dr. Manning's lab?" Emily asked, her eyes wide with amazement—and surprise. "What did they steal?"

"I'm not at liberty to say," Kat hedged, wondering herself what the kids had taken, "but he's hired me to try to find the vandals. All he wants is his goods re-turned and no questions will be asked."

Emily held her arms out to her side. "So?"

"So you don't know anything about that either?"

Her sister's eyes blazed with anger. "I just told you that I don't know anything about any vandalism."

"I have to ask."

"Because you're a private detective, right?"

"No," Kat said. "Because you're my sister and I don't want to see you getting into trouble."

"Right." Emily stood, arms crossed, looking angry. At least she hadn't stomped upstairs.

Kat tried to think of something to say to ease the tension between them. She wanted to demand Em come up with alibis for both incidents, but she backed off, maybe because she was afraid of what Emily was hiding from her.

Em shook her head as she started to clean up the

spilled nachos. "I have homework to do." She looked up at Kat, obviously waiting for her to say something. Or maybe apologize.

"I'll help you clean up the nachos," Kat said. "Maybe we could make another batch. I wouldn't mind a few." She saw Emily weaken a little.

"I can clean up my own mess."

"You know I love you."

"Right," Em said, sighing. "And you worry about me. And you only give me a hard time because you're older and you don't want me to make some of the same mistakes you've made."

That about summed it up. "Yes. Sure you don't want more nachos? I'd share with you."

Em shook her head, her back to Kat, as she rose and took the dirty plate to the kitchen. Kat could hear water running in the sink, the slam of the trash can. Kat turned on the TV to the late news.

A few minutes later, Emily came out of the kitchen with a fresh plate of nachos. Wordlessly, she handed them to Kat. "I got a job today. At the ice-cream shop. I thought you'd like that."

Kat smiled. "I do."

Em nodded and smiled grudgingly. "Like, how much trouble can I get into at an ice-cream shop?"

Kat didn't want to even think. "Let me know if you need any help with your homework, and thanks for the nachos," she said, touched by her sister's thoughtfulness.

"Yeah, you're a real whiz at calculus. Like you would be of any help." She rewarded her with a small smile as she headed upstairs.

The phone rang and Emily hurried back down to pick it up.

"It's Angela," Em mouthed, motioning that she would take the cordless phone upstairs.

Kat nodded, figuring Angela had called to patch things up after their fight. "You're in for the night, though, right?"

Emily turned to give Kat an impatient look. "I'm not going anywhere. I told you I have calculus."

Kat channel surfed and nibbled on the chips for a while, then washed the plate and followed her sister on up to bed. It wasn't until she reached her third-floor bedroom that she realized why she'd avoided going to bed for so long. The nightmare. After everything that had happened tonight, all she needed was to have the dream again.

Without turning on the light, she went to open the French doors and step out into the night. Stars glittered overhead, the moon brighter and bigger. The fog hung in the trees of the town green.

Was it possible her brake line really had been cut, as Jonah had told her? She'd know in the morning when Doug at the garage took a look. In the meantime she'd remain skeptical and leery. It was too much of a coincidence that Jonah had been on that road tonight. Between him and Emily, she was worried. But Kat knew it was more than that. She felt...scared of the future. Why was that?

The town clock struck midnight. She thought of Dr. Manning and his missing research materials. Had they been returned before the witching hour?

A movement down by the witch-hanging tree caught her eye. She saw a man looking her way. He stepped back into the foliage and fog, but there was no mistaking who she'd seen. Jonah Ries. And there was no doubt he was watching her house.

Earlier, after their almost accident, she'd forgotten about asking him why he seemed to have an interest in her—and her mother's murder. Now he was watching her house....

Kat tapped at Em's door, waited a minute, then knocked again. No answer. She opened the door, thinking Emily was probably still on the phone and hadn't either heard the knock—or had ignored it.

The room was empty, the window open and the breeze stirring the note pinned to Em's pillow. "Sorry sis, but I have to talk to Angela. I'm spending the night at her house—in case you find this."

Kat swore under her breath, noting that Emily had failed to take her calculus book with her. But right now, Kat had something even more pressing to take care of. Jonah Ries.

Tired of being scared and in the dark about what was going on, she pulled the Beretta from her purse, determined to find out exactly what this man wanted from her—and why he was so sure someone was trying to kill her.

Chapter Eleven

Kat kept to the shadows as she moved through the darkness toward the tree. Behind it the gazebo glowed stark white in the illumination from the scant lights on the green.

She could no longer see Jonah under the witch tree but she knew he hadn't had time to cross the green and leave without her seeing him. He was here somewhere and she intended to find him.

The breeze smelled of the sea, sharp and cold as the Atlantic was this time of year. In the distance, the foghorn moaned soulfully. The dark seemed to close around her.

She saw Jonah before he saw her. He had started past the gazebo, then stopped and moved toward it as if drawn there. He didn't seem aware of her as she cut across the green after him.

As she drew closer, she saw that he knelt over something at the back of the gazebo on one of the benches. She slowed her steps, a vague sense of unease turning into something much worse.

A white object caught her eye. White like daisy petals. White like seagull wings. On a gust of breeze, it billowed out. White like the scarf that had been tied around her mother's neck.

And that's when she saw the body.

JONAH SWUNG AROUND, startled by the shrill blood-curdling scream. He hadn't heard Kat approach—nor had he sensed her presence. He'd been too shocked at what he'd seen lying in the gazebo—lying in the exact spot Leslie Ridgemont had lain.

Hurriedly, he tried to shield Kat from the body lying naked on the bench with the white silk scarf knotted around its throat.

Kat stumbled back, the fear in her expression almost dropping him to his knees. She thought he'd killed the woman lying there.

"Easy," he said, trying to calm her. "It isn't what you think."

But from the wild, terrified look in her eyes, she wasn't hearing him. She was reliving her mother's murder. The thought tore at him. He could have killed the person with his bare hands who'd done this, because there was no doubt in his mind that it had been for Kat's benefit.

"It's a prank," he said, reaching for her.

She stepped back from his touch, shaking her head.

"It's a cadaver, probably stolen from the college as part of some fraternity thing," he said, although he couldn't imagine a more cruel prank. The cadaver, smelling of formaldehyde and obviously lacking in blood, had been placed in the same spot as Kat's mother had been found twenty years ago, complete with the deadly white scarf around its neck. Jonah

knew it was no prank. It was a warning. Pure and simple. ''I've called the police.''

Her gaze came up to meet his then, her eyes still
filled with terror and what he suspected were flashes
of memory.

He reached for her again. This time she didn't try to
move away from him. Pulling her into his arms, he held
her tightly, afraid she might break if he let her go. In
the distance he could hear the police siren.

KAT WRAPPED the blanket around her shoulders, still
chilled to her core. She felt too shocked to make any
sense of the things that had happened tonight, too tired
to even try.

Across the interrogation room at the police department, Jonah stood leaning against the wall, looking relaxed to all appearances. But she could see the tension
in his face, in his large masculine hands, as he sipped
a cup of the hot horrible station coffee and seemed to
wait patiently. She had felt his gaze, almost as com-
forting as his arms had been.

''Thank you,'' Cullen Ryan said, and hung up the
phone, jotting down a couple of notes before he looked
up at her. Kat had known Cullen since they were kids
growing up in Moriah's Landing. At six feet, with short
dark hair and an edgy, confident manner, he'd once
been the town's bad boy, living in a section of town
almost as ill-reputed as where the Rieses had lived.

But he'd become a cop, returned to town and fallen
madly in love with her best friend, Elizabeth Douglas.
They were to be married in little over a week and Kat

was going to be her maid of honor. But right now, none of that seemed real.

"The body you found," Cullen said, "has been identified and claimed. It's a cadaver Dr. Manning was using for research at his laboratory."

"A cadaver," she repeated.

Cullen nodded. "It was one of the bodies donated to Dr. Manning for his research. He says it was stolen sometime last night."

That was the property he'd hired her to get back? No wonder he hadn't wanted to tell her.

"That doesn't explain how it ended up in the gazebo on the town green with a white scarf tied around its neck," Jonah said, sounding angry.

Cullen eyed Jonah with a guarded expression. "Nor does it explain what you were doing on the green tonight kneeling over the body."

"I told you, I was cutting through the park on my way to talk to Ms. Ridgemont when I saw something move in the gazebo, obviously the scarf. I had just found the body when Ms. Ridgemont discovered me."

Just cutting through the park? A clear lie, Kat thought. She felt Cullen's gaze swing to her.

"You have any idea who might have done this?"

She shook her head. She'd been so sure that Razz and Dodie had stolen Dr. Manning's "property" and that they would return it for the reward—not use it for some malicious prank.

"We'll continue to look for the person or persons who did this," Cullen assured her. "In the meantime, the cadaver is being returned to Dr. Manning. I'm sorry you had to see it, though, Kat."

She nodded and got to her feet, leaving the blanket he'd given her on the chair.

"I'll see you home," Jonah said, taking her arm.

"I don't want you going home alone at this hour," Cullen said, watching Jonah with suspicion. As bad as Cullen's family had been, it paled in comparison with the Rieses. No doubt he was worried about her. And with good reason. "I could give you a ride," Cullen offered.

Kat smiled, even more happy that Elizabeth had found him. "Thanks, but Mr. Ries can take me home." She had no intention of letting Jonah take her anywhere. She just wanted him alone, away from the police station.

Jonah seemed surprised—and wary that she'd opt to let him take her home. Smart man.

Once outside the police station, they walked the half block to the edge of the park where Jonah had left his motorcycle earlier. A breeze moved through the trees, scattering the fog among the branches. It rose in wisps, free as lost spirits. At this time of the morning, the streets were deserted and dark. She and Jonah were alone.

"Okay," she said, stopping at the edge of light from one of the quaint old street lamps. "Let's have it."

He turned to look at her, surprised by her tone, no doubt. Even more surprised by the Beretta in her hand. "The truth. Why is it that every time I turn around I find myself tripping over you? Why were you watching my house last night? What are you doing in Moriah's Landing?"

He just stared at her.

"Hello?" She sounded like Emily.

Slowly, he shook his head. "What I have to tell you might come as a shock."

"At this point, nothing you could tell me could shock me."

"I wouldn't count on that," he said, his voice a low rumble that reverberated through her. His look could have melted stone.

She felt herself shiver. "Try me."

"I'm working undercover with the FBI."

Whew. She'd pretty much guessed that. Or at least suspected it. For a moment, she thought he was going to tell her—

"That's the good part," he said quietly. "Being a Ries comes with a small quirk, like I tried to tell you earlier. Because of my genes, I'm considered a warlock."

She stared at him. He was joking. Sure, she'd heard stories about the Ries family, weird, creepy stories, but Jonah was different, Jonah was—"Let me guess, something to do with the full moon and wolves?"

"That's a *werewolf.*"

She knew that. She'd been joking. "Then I guess you'd better tell me what being considered a warlock has to do with why you were watching my house last night, why you've been asking around town about me—and my mother's murder."

"It means that I can sometimes…sense things," he said, his voice low.

"You mean like gut instinct?" She could relate to that.

He shook his head. "More like…psychic stuff."

Get out of here. "You don't expect me to believe—"

"Here in Moriah's Landing my psychic ability is stronger than it was when I was gone." His eyes met hers. "It's stronger around you."

Right. A thought struck her. "Are you telling me you can read my mind?" She didn't like the sound of this. If he could read her mind, then he knew how she'd been thinking about him. She felt her face flush at the thought.

"No, I can't read your mind."

She couldn't believe her relief. But then, she didn't believe any of this, did she? "If you can't read minds…"

"It's hard to explain," he was saying.

She was sure it was.

"I just get strong feelings sometimes." He shrugged.

"That's it?" She hadn't meant to sound disappointed.

His gaze narrowed. "What did you expect?"

"I'd at least expect some superhero powers," she said. She put the Beretta away, knowing that she didn't need it with Jonah. A warlock. Oh yeah.

"You aren't taking this seriously."

She smiled. Maybe he *could* read her mind. "If you really were psychic you'd be at the nearest horse track making your next million."

"It doesn't work that way either." He sounded disgusted. With her or with himself, she wasn't sure. "Look, I'm only telling you this so you understand—"

"Understand what?" she said, her own antennae going up.

He ran his tongue over his upper lip, the movement drawing attention to his mouth, making her realize again just how dangerous this man really was to her.

He looked away for a moment, then back at her, the intensity of his gaze practically nailing her to the brick sidewalk. "Could we go somewhere and talk about this? It isn't something I think we should discuss out here on the street." He reached for her, his touch like a live wire on her skin. "As I tried to tell you earlier, you're in danger."

She pulled back, suddenly wanting to cry. "Don't do this, okay? You're scaring me." She felt her heart take off at a dead run. "If you're working with the FBI, it can't be on my mother's case, not a twenty-year-old murder, unless..." She stared at him, his expression making her suddenly bone-chilled cold.

"I think her killer is after *you* now," Jonah said quietly, painfully. "I think he has been for some time."

No. She looked past him, the moon bright. Everything in her wanted to argue that he was wrong. But hadn't she felt something? Still... "If someone really was after me, then what is he waiting for?"

"The full moon."

The full moon? For a moment there, she'd almost started to believe him a little. *"The full moon?"*

"Trust me on this," he said. "We have forty-eight hours to find him. I'm going to need your help."

"Hold on. Without some sort of evidence, how do I know any of this is real or that anything you've told me is the truth?"

"You know," he said softly, his gaze holding hers as he drew her toward the motorcycle.

She went, her mind rebelling, and yet part of her kept thinking of the daisies. Those damn daisies. If it wasn't for them and the trouble with her car tonight...

He handed her the helmet off the seat of his bike and climbed on, waiting for her to do the same.

Slipping on the helmet, she swung her leg over the seat, trying to stay back, away from him, as if by not touching him she could distance herself from what he'd told her. Distance herself from the impact this man had on her.

It proved impossible. She slid down the leather until her front was pressed against his back. His touch brought on all the conflicting emotions she'd felt since the first night she'd met him. As if she didn't have enough problems.

"Hang on," he said as he started the engine and gave it gas. The bike leaped into noisy motion. She threw her arms around his waist to keep from falling off, reinforcing contact. She closed her eyes, giving up, too tired to fight the chemistry between them.

The ride to her house was, thankfully, short, the cool night air clearing her head a little.

He pulled the motorcycle up to the front door. She started to get off the bike, wanting to break the physical contact as quickly as possible, but Jonah reached back to put a stilling hand on her thigh. He motioned toward the dark porch. Her front door stood open.

Chapter Twelve

"Could your sister have left the door open?" Jonah whispered, easing off the bike seat as he pulled the .38 from his shoulder holster.

"No." As she slipped off the seat, he saw she had her weapon in her hand again. Just his luck getting involved with a private eye. Especially one who looked like this one.

It wasn't as if he hadn't noticed the way her jeans hugged her hips and molded her wonderful round bottom. The white fabric of the crop top lay stark against her olive skin. Her belly was brown above her jeans, and he'd caught the small flash of silver when she moved toward the porch. A belly-button ring?

She gave him a look that told him not to say a word about her going into the house with him.

He motioned to her to at least stay behind him. Carefully, he climbed the porch and eased the front door open a little farther, listening for any sounds in the house. When he heard none, he moved inside, waiting before he flicked on the flashlight from his pocket.

He moved swiftly through the lower floor. While the front door lock had been jimmied open, the rest of the house looked undisturbed—and almost too quiet. It obviously hadn't been a burglary or the thieves weren't interested in the TV, stereo, DVD player or the silver.

He felt an odd sensation and stopped, his breath catching. The person who'd broken in hadn't come to take something—but to leave something. And that person had left the door open on purpose. He'd wanted Kat to know he'd been there. Just as he'd left the cadaver in the gazebo.

Jonah rushed back toward the front of house. No Kat. Upstairs, a floorboard creaked. He swore and, taking two stairs at a time, raced up to the second level.

He didn't find her there, so kept going up to the third floor, bursting into her bedroom. Past her he could see the widow's walk where she'd stood earlier tonight. Where he sensed she'd stood the night of her mother's murder.

She didn't seem to hear him come racing in. Nor did she answer when he said her name. She stood in front of the vanity, holding something in the palm of her hand, looking at if she'd seen a ghost. And he knew. She'd found what the intruder had left for her.

THE MOMENT SHE WALKED into the room, Kat had smelled her mother's perfume, the scent so strong, so overpowering she fought to breathe. Memories swamped her, pulling her under, the memories of her mother tightly caught up in the scent of her perfume.

It was as if her mother had just been in the room, her perfume lingering behind. Just as her sordid reputation and the odd circumstances of her death had.

At first she'd thought she was only imagining the

scent, the same way she could imagine her mother in this room, sitting at her dressing table, putting on her lipstick getting ready to go to work. Kat had hated it when her mother went to work. Hated the smell of that perfume. It meant her mother wouldn't be home until late because she'd be meeting a man after work. A man who wasn't Kat's daddy. Where had that memory come from?

Kat had moved to the dressing table, catching her reflection in the mirror, startled to see her mother's face—not her own. It was as if Leslie Ridgemont had come back from the grave.

As she stumbled back, she hit the edge of the vanity. Something glasslike tumbled over, drawing her attention. It was a small lavender bottle with a glass rose on the cork stopper. A perfume bottle.

Her pulse thundered in her ears as she reached for it. Some of the perfume had spilled out on the vanity top. She cradled the tiny lavender bottle in her palm, just as she imagined her mother had years ago.

"Kat?" Jonah's voice sounded far away.

The perfume bottle was like the one her mother used to have. The one Kat had thrown away when she'd found it in her mother's things.

She stared at the bottle in her palm, the cloying scent making her sick to her stomach. It hadn't been on the vanity this morning. She would have remembered. Someone had left it here for her, pushing everything else aside on the vanity so she couldn't miss it. Just as she couldn't miss the front door standing open when she came home.

"Kat!" Jonah said next to her.

She blinked, the spell broken.

"What's wrong?" Jonah asked, his voice tense.

She looked over at him, remembering everything he'd told her and how she hadn't wanted to believe him that she was in danger, that someone was after her. "It's the same perfume my mother used to wear."

"Here, give it to me," he said, frowning with concern as he pulled a tissue from the box at the edge of the vanity and took the bottle carefully from the palm of her hand. "Do you have a plastic bag we can put it in?"

She nodded, still shocked that someone had broken into her house to leave the perfume where she would find it. Just as they'd left the daisies. Just as they'd left the cadaver. Only this time, they'd come inside her house. Into her bedroom.

She felt herself begin to shake. Felt Jonah's arm around her shoulders. She stepped into him for a moment, soaking up his warmth, his strength, his arms coming around her to hold her tightly. Then she straightened and went to get a bag for the evidence. Evidence.

She no longer believed she had nothing to fear. Or that she could handle this alone.

JONAH MADE HER WARM MILK and insisted she sit in the overstuffed chair in the living room. He'd closed the curtains, locked the door and told her he wasn't leaving her alone, but he could tell she didn't feel safe. He knew she didn't trust him. But then, why should she?

She drank the milk. He thought maybe some of the

warmth might have eased the chill inside her—the same chill he felt.

"Who are you?" she asked, not looking at him.

The question surprised him. "I already told you."

"Right, you're a warlock. With no powers. Just the ability to 'know' certain things. Funny, but before I met you, none of this was happening. No daisies on my doorstep, no one following me home, no one spying on me, no one breaking into my house."

He could hear the fear in her voice. She hadn't taken him seriously before, but now she was scared.

"I'm not the one doing this," he said.

"You just 'sense' the person who is." He could see that she was fighting tears. She waved her hand through the air, her gaze settling on him. "I didn't feel afraid until you came to town," she said, her voice breaking.

"I don't blame you for being…skeptical," he said.

"I'm a lot more than skeptical," she retorted. "I want to know everything. What you're doing here in Moriah's Landing, everything. Including a name of someone I can talk to at the FBI to verify that you're for real."

That could be a small problem. "If you call the FBI they will tell you my cover story—that I was kicked out."

She started to rise from the chair, her gaze going to her purse and the Beretta he'd seen her slide back inside it.

"Hold on," he said, realizing what he was about to tell her could get them both killed. But at this point, he feared neither of them had much more to lose.

She sat back down.

"A month ago, one of our agents came to Moriah's Landing undercover," he said. "The FBI had received an anonymous note that some illegal medical supplies were coming in by boat. That agent disappeared. I've been sent here to find out what happened to him—and intercept another boat, this one, according to our anonymous informant, carrying yet another shipment of these same illegal supplies."

"What are they?" she asked.

He shook his head. "We suspect it has something to do with the secret society of scientists that dates back to the first residents in this town."

She nodded, no doubt having heard the rumors of the secret society. "And the agent? You're assuming he's dead?"

"Yes. Max would have checked in by now if he hadn't been." Jonah couldn't hide his guilt.

"And you got involved with me because I mistook you for my blind date," she said.

"At first. Then I realized you were in danger." Even now he couldn't be sure that his showing up hadn't had some effect on the killer's plans for Kat.

"If you can 'sense' this, why can't you 'sense' the killer?" she asked. "And tell me who he is so I can stop him?"

"It's not an exact science," he said. "Some people think it's a gift. I'm not one of them. But it is definitely a case of use it or lose it. I haven't used it since I left here. This may surprise you, but I was tired of being different. I didn't want to know about the things going on around me so I worked hard at not feeling—or knowing anything."

"So this gift of yours is rusty, is what you're saying?" She studied him, disbelief in her eyes. And concern.

"And I'm here without any backup as part of my cover."

She didn't seem happy to hear this.

"All I can tell you is that the first night I met you I sensed someone out in the fog watching you, so I followed you home. Someone else followed you as well."

She blinked. "I thought I heard two sets of footsteps behind me."

He nodded. "I saw a man watching your house the next night. I chased him, but lost him in the cemetery. Unfortunately, I didn't get close enough that I could see his face."

"You do realize how this all sounds," she said, getting up from her chair to go to the window. She pushed aside the curtain.

"I know you don't want to believe me. Or trust me," he said. "But I think part of you does. It isn't just the daisies and the perfume, is it?"

She turned slowly. He met the heat of her gaze. As always, it sent a jolt through him. He saw her weaken a little, unsure.

"There's been something else, hasn't there?" he said quietly.

She brushed her hair back from her face. "I'm having the nightmare again," she said, her voice barely a whisper. "It's the same one I had after my mother died, disjointed, frightening, too mixed up to make much sense of." She seemed to hesitate.

"Something has changed in the dream?"

She nodded, not seeming overly surprised that he knew that. Or had guessed it. "Blood. I saw blood."

The thing that had started the rumors about a vampire killer on the town green.

"I know it doesn't make any sense—"

"It does make sense, Kat. I've seen the official report. Your mother had two small cuts on her neck. The police believed that the killer strangled her until she was unconscious then took some of her blood. He was interrupted, possibly by Arabella, or he might have taken more."

Kat closed her eyes. "Claire's blood was also taken when he had her." He could see that for twenty years she'd feared her mother's killer was still out there. Maybe even feared that the man had taken the wrong woman that night in the cemetery five years ago. Maybe he'd been after Kat all along and mistakenly had kidnapped Claire.

"It wasn't the same man."

Kat's head snapped up. "What?"

"I don't think the man who killed your mother and the one who abducted Claire were the same men," he said.

"How can you be sure of that?" she demanded.

"I can't. It's just a…feeling I have, and admittedly, not a very strong one," he conceded.

Jonah knew it definitely wasn't Dr. Rathfastar, the man responsible for the deaths in Moriah's Landing earlier this year, who'd been stalking Kat. He was dead. Nor had he been around back when Claire was attacked.

"Why now?" she asked, sounding scared. "Next

you're going to tell me that you think this has something to do with the twentieth anniversary of my
mother's death. Or even the 350th anniversary of the
town.''

''Not in the way you mean. This is no ghost after
you. A lot of factors could be contributing to the killer
making his move now. The fact that you look so much
like your mother, that you're about the age she was
when she died...'' The moon. But he didn't tell her
that. ''There is one other possibility,'' he said cautiously. ''You were three when your mother died,
right?''

She nodded.

''So you weren't alone in the house,'' he said.

''My father was at sea, my mother at work, my
grandmother was baby-sitting me.''

''Were you living in this house?''

She nodded.

The crucial question. ''Where was your bedroom?''

''On the second floor.''

Her answer threw him. If his instincts about this
were off, then what did that say about the others? ''You
were asleep on the second floor then at the time of the
murder?''

She started to nod, then stopped. ''No, I forgot. I
had a bad dream. My grandmother told me she put me
in bed with her. She was staying in my mother's
room.''

His heart leaped. ''In your mother's room on the
third floor, the bedroom with the widow's walk?''

She nodded.

Jonah let out a sigh. ''Kat, I think you saw your

mother's murderer that night from the widow's walk.''
He hesitated. ''I think he saw you as well.''

KAT STARED AT HIM, her pulse thudding in her ears.
Part of her actually believed him. Why was that?

''I believe you woke up that night and went to the
widow's walk. There was a full moon that night. But
it was raining. Still you could have seen him either
going into the gazebo with your mother or coming back
out later.''

She stared into Jonah's dark eyes, seeing the night
as he pictured it.

''I think he saw you there,'' Jonah said. ''But because you were so young—''

''He didn't think I would ever remember.'' Her eyes
widened as she had a thought. ''The nightmare. You
think I'm starting to remember.''

He didn't say a word but she knew that's exactly
what he thought. ''But he couldn't possibly know
about the nightmare—'' She stopped in midthought.
''There was this one night. I was having the nightmare
and I woke up. I thought I smelled my mother's perfume. But I also thought someone was in the room, but
by the time my eyes adjusted to the light...''

She could see the possibility freaked him. If it was
true, it wasn't the first time the killer had been in her
house, in her bedroom. She shivered and hugged herself as the ramifications finally caught up with her.

Had she repressed memories of her mother's murder? Or was it just a bad dream and nothing more?

The tears seemed to come out of nowhere. Frustra-
tion and fear. It was inconceivable that someone would

want to kill her. And more than likely just because she looked like her mother.

"This is just so…unreal," she said, her throat tight with tears.

Jonah started to get up, to comfort her, she was sure. She knew if he touched her, she wouldn't be able to hold back the tears, and right now she needed to be strong. She needed to be able to take care of herself. Leaning on any man right now would be a mistake. Leaning on Jonah Ries could be the worst mistake she could make.

She moved to the phone by the front door. "I have to be sure Emily is all right." She dialed her sister's best friend's number. Angela's mother answered after three rings.

"Emily? She isn't here, Kat. Angela's grounded until after graduation and can't have any sleepovers. Maybe she's staying at another friend's."

Kat asked to speak to Angela. "Do you know where Emily is?"

"She's in the bathroom right now, but I can have her call you," Angela said, not realizing their cover had been blown.

"Try again. Your mother just told me that Emily never had any plans to spend the night at your house. Where is she?"

"I don't know. *Really*. She just told me to cover for her."

Kat hung up, more upset than ever.

"Your sister?" Jonah asked.

"She's not at a sleepover like she told me," she said.

"I'm worried that she's running with the wrong bunch of kids."

He stepped to her so quickly, she didn't have time to deflect his comfort. He pulled her to him. She leaned into him, letting him hold her, seduced by the warmth of his body, by a gentleness she saw in the deep brown of his eyes, all the time telling herself it was wrong. But how could she not believe he possessed special powers? Look at the power he had over her body. Over her emotions. And now, over her life.

JONAH PULLED BACK, frowning as he suddenly realized something had changed between them.

She caught his arm to keep him from moving away from her and shook her head. "Don't."

"Kat—"

She touched a fingertip to his lips. "If you really can feel things that the rest of us can't…"

He looked into her eyes. It didn't take a mind reader for this one. "Are you sure?" he had to ask. Just like on their first date, she looked nervous, definitely scared.

His gaze met hers, pulling her in as his hand reached to cup her cheek. He saw her take a breath and let it out slowly, her eyes wide with fear, her body tense.

"Tell me what you sense about me right now," she whispered.

He studied her face, her request too easy. "You want me to kiss you again."

She took another breath, this one catching in her throat, but she nodded slightly, her eyes locked with his.

"That isn't all you want me to do," he said, surprised how rough his voice sounded. "You want me to make you forget—just for a little while." His heart thundered in his chest. He couldn't remember ever feeling like this, as if he were about to plunge off a cliff—even though he knew there would be no turning back, he couldn't wait to jump.

Kat let out a sigh. "You can read my mind after all," she whispered. Her eyes were liquid blue, her gaze as determined as he'd ever seen it.

"Then why are you so afraid?"

She shook her head. "Kiss me. Please."

He glanced down at her lips, felt her tremble. Her mouth pulled at him like the moon pulled at him. He covered her mouth with his own, her lips soft and warm.

Then he felt the tentative touch of her tongue and he was engulfed with a desire so strong, he felt his insides clench.

He stepped back, holding her at arm's length. "I can't do this."

"Is it me?" She looked as though she might cry.

He shook his head. "It's the man who hurt you."

She seemed startled. She bit her lip for a moment as if holding back emotions she'd had bottled up for a long time. "I made a mistake a few years go." She started to cry, the words coming hard. "He…he hurt me—physically and emotionally."

Jonah silenced her with a finger to her lips. "I know."

She didn't question how he knew. Her eyes overflowed with tears.

"I'm so sorry. But it wasn't your fault." He pulled

her to him again, encircling her in his arms, her body small and fragile. He could feel her jerking, hear her muffled sobs.

Everything in him wanted to protect her from now until eternity. But he was smart enough to know he wouldn't be there. She would want someone very different from him. She didn't know it, but the day would come when she'd want a painted white house that overlooked the ocean and three kids playing out in the yard. He could never give her that.

It took him a moment to still the anger he felt for the man who'd hurt her. He gave her the time she needed as well.

Then he drew back, wiped her tears with a tissue and, cupping her face in his hands, looked into her eyes. He could no more not kiss her than not take his next breath.

The kiss was long and sweet, slow and easy. He slid his hand along the bare skin between her jeans and cotton top. Her flesh felt warm, as inviting as a dip in the Atlantic, as his fingertips ran up the hollow of her back. No bra. He pulled her closer and felt her sigh against him, her body softening into him, her bare breasts beneath the crop top full and firm.

Her skin felt sun-warm and smooth. Her lips parted in invitation as a small gasp escaped, and he felt her tremble against him, this time with desire rather than fear.

"Please, Jonah," she whispered against his mouth.

Or maybe he just heard it in his head.

He pulled back to look into all that blue, now bright

with desire, his own body alive with the feel of her, the need for her.

"Kat, someday you're going to want more than I can give you," he said, holding her at arm's length.

"All I want is you now. It might be all we have."

Didn't he know it. He took her in his arms. At least they had the rest of the night.

KAT HAD ALREADY KNOWN what Jonah could do to her senses. She'd only imagined what he could do to her body. But she'd had no idea what he could do to her heart.

He carried her up the stairs and laid her gently on the bed. Then he lay down beside her and slowly began to make love to her with his mouth, his hands, his body.

It was as if she'd never made love before. She gave herself, surrendering to him with heart and soul. There was no turning back. She'd known that the moment she'd seen the hurt in his eyes when she'd told him about her disastrous past relationship.

She had never felt more love for anyone than at that moment. Nor had she realized the extent to which she'd blamed herself for that earlier mistake.

Jonah kissed away her fears, caressing away the hurt and pain, showing her what lovemaking should be. Tender. Sweet. Wonderful. It was as if he knew exactly what she wanted, what she needed, what would make her capable of loving again.

When it was over, she curled in his arms, warm against him, and slept, safe. For a few hours, she forgot there was a killer after her. For a few hours, she could lean on Jonah Ries.

WHEN KAT WOKE to the sun, the bed beside her was empty, but she knew Jonah wasn't gone. She put on her robe and went downstairs. She heard the sound of the shower running and thought for a moment about joining him.

But she felt strangely shy, remembering the wonderful things he'd done to her, the emotions he'd elicited with just a touch, a word, a look. She started toward the kitchen, planning to make coffee, when the doorbell rang.

Emily? Had she forgotten her key? Or had she seen Jonah's motorcycle and thought she'd better ring the bell first?

Kat hurried to the door, upset with her sister. But when she opened it, there was no one waiting on the porch. At first all she saw was Jonah's bike, lying on its side where someone had knocked it over. It startled her and scared her at the same time.

Then she looked down and saw the daisies, the same type of bouquet she'd been getting, tied with another piece of worn red ribbon. Only these daisies looked as if someone had stomped them viciously with a boot heel.

JONAH CAME OUT of the bathroom in his jeans, a towel in his hand, and saw Kat in the doorway. He could tell that something was wrong and rushed to her. The moment he saw his bike, he knew. He didn't need to see the daisies crushed on the doorstep.

"It's okay," he said, reaching for her. Her reaction surprised him.

"It's not okay," she snapped, turning around to

glare at him. "I'm damn tired of being scared. That's what he's trying to do, you know. Scare me. If he had any guts at all he'd just come after me and get it over with."

Jonah looked into her face and had to smile. He'd expected her to be in tears, running scared. Any woman would be at this point. But not Kat. She was coming out fighting.

"The bastard put the same bouquet on my mother's casket," she said.

Jonah felt a jolt. "How do you know that?"

She closed the door and went into the other room, coming back with a newspaper clipping. Jonah stared at the bouquet in the photo, then at her.

"Kat, you know this man," he said. "He's someone in this town, someone your mother knew." Jonah could feel the man's desperate desire for Kat, the same desire he'd had for her mother—but nothing more. If only that sense of knowing would let him see the man's face.

"I'm going to find him."

"*We're* going to find him," he corrected her. He had a couple of thoughts on where they could start. But first he needed to bag the daisies. Even though he doubted the lab could get prints off the ribbon, he had to try. They had thirty-six hours before the moon was full. Time was running out.

KAT LOOKED at the list of suspects—those people who had been seen on the town green that night near the time of the murder. "You think it's one of them?"

Jonah nodded. "We know it's a man, so that narrows it down some."

"You can't just look at this list and 'sense' which one?" she asked, only half joking.

He shook his head.

"Well, until I see these powers at work, you don't mind if I remain skeptical?"

He smiled then, a real smile. "I would be disappointed if you didn't."

She looked down at the list in her hand. Until last night, Kat had discounted what Jonah thought, discounted his concern for her because she didn't trust him. No, she thought, because she didn't believe in his instincts or legends about ghosts or witches or...warlocks. And she was scared to death of the way she felt when she was around him because of her attraction to him.

She looked up at Jonah, realizing with a jolt that she was now trusting his instincts—and not just because of what they had shared last night. "You think this guy could have left her bouquets of daisies before he killed her?"

Jonah nodded. "I think he had a thing for her, a secret crush, maybe. For whatever reason, he was afraid to tell her. Maybe he was too young for her or too old, or was too poor or too rich."

She felt cold inside. "Then he could have been any one of these men. Men who were too young for her, like Brody Ries and Marley Glasglow. Or men whose social standing would never have allowed them to "love" her outright, like Geoffrey Pierce or Dr. Leland Manning or even Ernie McDougal."

Jonah nodded. "There is someone else who might have seen the killer that night as well. Arabella Leigh."

For just a moment, Kat had been hopeful. "Arabella's been out of her head for years."

"Even before your mother's murder?"

Kat nodded and glanced at her watch. "I have to find my sister and go to my office—at least for a little while." She could see that he didn't want her out of his sight, but it was also clear that he had things to do. And it was daylight, and if he was right, she had nothing to fear until tomorrow night when the moon was finally full. It was also time for her to stand on her own two feet for a while. Hopefully, he sensed that.

She started to head for the stairs, but he pulled her to him, leaned down and kissed her, a slow, sweet, full-mouth kiss that made her knees weak. "Be careful."

"Always." She touched his face with her fingertips. "We have thirty-six hours. Between the two of us, we'll find him."

JONAH HOPED TO HELL she was right as he neared his apartment over the Wharf Rat, but he wasn't worried about her because his instincts told him the killer wouldn't hurt her until the moon was full.

The dental floss was still in the door where he'd left it. Once inside, he booted up his computer.

"I was worried," flashed on the screen. "Got a name on those prints. Sitting down?"

"Hit me." He'd managed to get Cassandra's glass last night out of the poker room and picked up by a courier to take to the print lab. But still he hadn't expected results this quickly.

"Cassandra Quintana—real name Sandra Langston.

Born Sandra Ries, daughter of Eli and Celia Ries. A relative?''

Jonah stared at the screen, pulse pounding, then slowly typed, ''Cousin.'' One he didn't know existed. His uncle Eli and aunt Celia had moved away before he was born. ''Record?''

''Just a driving-while-under-the-influence years ago.''

That would explain why they had her prints.

''Odd, though, Sandra used the name Ridgemont for a job reference twenty-two years ago. Leslie Ridgemont. Put her down as friend. Mean anything?''

Jonah let out a low whistle. ''Interesting.'' Boy, was that putting it mildly.

''Still no boat?''

''No.'' Nothing on their lost agent either. ''But have tour of Manning's lab tonight.''

''Maybe we'll get lucky.''

Why did he doubt that?

He typed, ''Later,'' then signed off, put the computer back under the sofa and locked up on his way out.

CASSANDRA QUINTANA, aka Sandra Ries Langston, had hooked a sucker. From a distance, Jonah watched her turn the tarot cards. A middle-aged woman with dyed blond hair and a Florida tan listened intently as Cassandra read the cards in a soft and serious hypnotic tone.

Whatever Cassandra was saying, the middle-aged woman was eating it up. He wondered what was missing in the woman's life that Cassandra was now promising her. Money? A man? Happiness?

The woman thanked the fortune-teller, laying a couple of twenties on the velvet. Cassandra scooped up the money as quickly as she did the cards.

"You're good," he said, stepping in front of her booth as she shuffled the deck. "But then, you come by it naturally."

She looked up as if she'd known he was there. She probably did, given her genes. But it could just be her talent for noticing even the smallest of things—and using them to her advantage.

"Why didn't you tell me who you were?" he demanded, keeping his voice down. He didn't need to advertise another Ries relative, not after years of trying to distance himself from the whole clan. Or coven, in this case.

She lifted an eyebrow and continued shuffling the tarot cards. "Maybe I don't want anyone to know who I am any more than you do."

He could buy that. "The best way to do that is stay as far from Moriah's Landing as possible—not come back here."

"Exactly."

"Want to tell me what brought you back here after all these years?" he asked, ignoring her implied question.

"Maybe I missed my roots."

Yeah, right.

"And you?"

He shrugged. "I didn't have anywhere else to go after the feds gave me the boot."

She smiled. "Maybe you can get a bonehead like

Brody to believe that, but I'm from the smart side of the Ries family. The...*sensitive* side.''

"Or at least that's what you want people to believe," he said, wondering how much of her psychic ability was a con—and how much just might be real.

She flipped over a card on the velvet. The lovers card and lifted an eyebrow. "You're right. She is in danger."

He didn't even blink an eye. "Who?"

Cassandra smiled. "Kat. And it does have to do with the sins of the mother. Interesting that the two of you have that in common."

He clenched his fists, trying to still the anger at even the mention of his mother. His mother had fallen in love with a Ries, knowing he had the "gift." Because her side of the family had their own bewitching talents, Jonah got a double whammy. They had given him the "gift," but it had killed them both, just as he suspected it would kill him one day. If he let it. Was it any wonder he'd fought it all these years? But now it was the one thing that would let him know how to save Kat and, ironically, it was too weak to sense just exactly who the killer was who was after her.

He looked at Cassandra, wondering if it was possible that she knew.

She flipped over another card, but before it could hit the velvet he covered it and her hand with his own.

"No more cards," he said from between gritted teeth. "No more games. Tell me who he is."

She shook her head. "You know as well as I do how the gift works." Gift his foot. It was a curse. She pushed his hand aside and looked down at the card lying on the table. "It is someone who feels betrayed by her." Cassandra met his gaze. "That is all I can tell you."

"You were a friend of Leslie's," he said. "You must have some idea. I know it's a man who was attracted to her—and felt betrayed by her."

"A lot of men were attracted to her—and were betrayed by her." Cassandra shrugged. "She was my friend, but I hated the way she behaved. I couldn't save her."

He heard the guilt in her voice. Is that why she'd come back to Moriah's Landing? To help Kat? He started to turn away, but she grabbed his wrist.

"You can stop him," she whispered. "But only if you stop fighting who you are, what you are. It is your birthright. Otherwise, you will die and so will this woman you have fallen in love with."

Chapter Thirteen

Kat stopped at Doug's Garage and Towing on her way to her office. She found Doug under the rack looking up under her car.

"Did you figure out what was wrong with it?" she asked, stepping under the car with him.

Doug squinted over at her from behind dirty safety glasses. He had gone to work with his dad at the garage right out of high school and was several years older than Kat.

"No mystery there," he said. "The line was cut clean as a whistle."

Jonah had been right.

"The power-steering fluid container has a puncture in it and the emergency-brake cable has been cut as well," Doug said, looking at her from behind the goggles, his eyes huge. "I also think they fooled with your clutch cable. Someone vandalized the hell out of your car."

"But I had some brakes last night. I used the emergency brake to stop. It couldn't have been cut all the way through."

Doug frowned. "Sorry, but both lines were cut all

the way through. I'm not sure how you got stopped but it wasn't with the emergency brake, I can tell you that much.''

She stared at him, feeling as if he'd just sucker punched her. If she hadn't had *any* brakes, then how had she avoided hitting Jonah?

CASSANDRA DIDN'T APPEAR in the least surprised to look up and find Kat standing in front of her booth. In fact, if Kat had believed in such things, she would have said the seer had been waiting for her to show up. But Kat hadn't even known she was coming here until her feet stopped outside the booth.

Cassandra nodded in greeting, motioning for her to come inside. In the back was a room that was small and warm, sweetly scented with candles and incense. Posters of the zodiacs leaped out from the brightly painted walls, each wall a different color. Books lined one wall, the titles covering everything from astrology to numerology. All for sale.

''You have come to have your cards read,'' Cassandra said, her dark gaze daring Kat to disagree.

''It's not that I believe for a minute that...'' She waved a hand through the air as she looked around the room, wondering what she *was* doing here.

''Please sit down,'' Cassandra said as if Kat hadn't spoken. The fortune-teller settled into the wide overstuffed chair in front of a tiny table, looking at home in this small, bright room. She picked up the worn cards and began to shuffle them with great care.

Kat told her legs to get her feet moving toward the door, but they stubbornly lowered her to the chair on the opposite side of the table, directly across from Cassandra.

Without a word, Cassandra handed her the surprisingly large deck of cards. They felt awkward in her hands and oddly cool to the touch.

"Ask the cards a question that can be answered with a yes or a no. As you shuffle the cards, think only of your question," Cassandra instructed in a singsong voice.

Kat found herself nodding as she mixed the cards, only one question on her mind this morning.

"Now cut the cards into three piles," the fortune-teller instructed. "Pick them up and give them to me."

As Kat handed her the cards again, she saw how serious Cassandra seemed, as if concentrating as well. Maybe on a question of her own?

Slowly, Cassandra turned over the first card. The Two of Cups. "This is your present situation concerning the question you asked. It has to do with love and passion and trust." She flipped over another card, the Six of Cups, and laid the card sideways across the first one. "These are past influences, memories from your childhood, that are hindering you and keeping you from what you want."

She flipped another card—the Three of Swords—and looked up at Kat, sympathy in her gaze. "You have been hurt in the past and have known great sorrow and disappointment." Kat cringed as Cassandra went on to describe the horrible, dangerous relationship Kat had been through.

Shaken, she leaned back in the chair.

The next card, the Page of Swords, depicted a person

from her recent past, Cassandra said. The meeting of a young man. A man with a message for her. A person adept at perceiving the unknown. A person alert to unknown dangers. Jonah.

"This card is your possible future," the seer said. "Remember, the future is not set in stone. You can still change it." She turned over the card. The Falling Tower.

Kat stared at the people falling from the tower in terror. "Do not despair," Cassandra said. "It is only a change card and signifies unexpected events. There are no bad cards."

Right, Kat thought. Tell that to the two figures depicted falling from the tower on the card, one a man and the other a woman.

The next card was the Ten of Cups. Kat stared at it, needing no explanation of its meaning. A woman, a man and a child held hands under a rainbow of cups.

"This represents your hopes and dreams. A home. Happiness. Love," Cassandra said, and turned over another card. "This is your immediate future." The card was the Knight of Swords. "It symbolizes bravery, heroic action, an impetuous rush into the unknown without fear. And, the final outcome."

Cassandra dropped the Seven of Wands. "You must overcome obstacles in your way, surmount overwhelming odds, but ultimately you can win."

Kat stared at the images on the velvet in front of her, wanting to believe. "How much do I owe you?" she asked, her voice sounded small, scared.

"Twenty-five," Cassandra said. "Cash."

Kat forked over the money as another woman came

up to the booth to have her fortune told. Somehow, the money put it all into perspective. She had been a fool to come here. No one knew the future. And it was better that way.

As Kat got to her feet, the seer folded the bills and stuffed them down into the neck opening of her caftan. ''He loves you. That is the question you wanted answered, yes?''

Kat stared at the woman for a shocked moment, then told herself that it had been an easy guess. Wasn't that what most women wanted to know? That, and how it would end?

''He would give his life for you,'' Cassandra continued. ''But he cannot give you children.'' Her dark gaze came up to meet Kat's startled one. ''As much as he loves you, he cannot bear to pass on the gift. And yet, if he does not, he will be cursed from the grave, never to know happiness.''

The words, as ridiculous as they were, sent a chill through her. Hadn't Jonah told her just last night that he could not give her what she wanted. And what she desperately wanted was a family.

KAT WORKED THE REST OF the day finishing up the paperwork on cases, answering phone messages and running credit checks for several of her clients, trying to keep her mind busy. Anything but thinking about the future—and what Cassandra had told her.

She had tried to reach Jonah at the bar but was told Brody had sent him out on business. She left a message, but by the end of the day he still hadn't called.

She was starting to worry about him, something she knew would do neither of them any good.

It was late when she finally quit working and let herself think about what had been happening to her the last few days—and what to do about it. Unlike Jonah she had no ESP or any paranormal abilities. She had to deal in hard evidence and in what she knew to be true.

She'd heard the footsteps behind her, two sets the night she met Jonah. That meant whoever had followed her home that first night had seen her with Jonah. Was that why the daisies had shown up on her office doorstep the next morning? Had the person decided to make himself known with the bouquet?

Following that line of reasoning, she could only assume the crushed daisies today and the tipped-over motorcycle indicated his unhappiness at seeing Jonah's bike parked in front of her house early in the morning. The anger she'd seen in the destroyed bouquet scared her. And what about the perfume on her mother's old vanity? A present? Or another warning that he could get to her at any time?

Unfortunately there was no way to trace the daisies. They grew wild almost everywhere. But the perfume...Kat opened the phone book to the local drugstore and dialed the number, hoping it was still open. It was a long shot he'd bought the scent locally and she knew it. But maybe he'd wanted to move quickly once he thought Jonah was in the picture.

"Do you happen to carry a perfume called Essence of Woman?" Kat asked when the clerk answered.

"Essence of Woman?"

"It comes in a small lavender bottle with a cork top that's shaped like a rose."

"Oh, that's from the Reminiscence Collection. I know which one you mean," she said. "Let me check. I remember we had one bottle. We normally don't even carry that brand, it's so expensive. I'm not sure if the person who ordered it ever came in and picked it up."

Kat held her breath. "It was a special order?"

"Yes, but I remember seeing it on the shelf," the clerk was saying. Kat could hear her rummaging around. "We put it out if it isn't picked up."

Kat waited, trying not to get her hopes up too high.

"I thought it was here.... Ethel, did you sell that bottle of Essence of Woman? You know, the cute little round one with the flower on top?"

"Sold it just yesterday," a woman called from somewhere in the store.

"She said—"

"I heard," Kat said, her heart racing. "Was it the person who special ordered it?"

The clerk called back the question.

"Nope. Gad, it's been so long since we placed that order I can't even remember who ordered it. Do you?"

The clerk said she didn't.

"Does she happen to remember who came in and bought it?" Kat interrupted.

"Who finally bought it?" the clerk called back.

Kat heard a laugh. "That Cavendish boy. There's so many of them I can't remember his name."

"The sullen fifteen-year-old with the blond spike haircut?" Kat suggested, and the clerk forwarded the question to Ethel.

"That's the one. Guess he's got himself a girl-friend," Ethel said with a cackle. "A girlfriend with expensive tastes."

"She said—"

"I heard. Thank you." Kat hung up, her hand trembling as she picked up her purse and went to find Tommy.

At the Bait & Tackle, she found Marley Glasglow closing up.

"I haven't seen the kid," Glasglow said with obvious disinterest. "Ernie's out on a charter, won't be back in until tomorrow evening."

She thanked him and left, feeling his gaze burning into her backside until she moved out of his range of sight. Pulling out her cell phone, she called the Wharf Rat. Still no Jonah. She asked to speak to Brody. He, too, was gone. She asked the bartender on duty if he'd seen Tommy Cavendish.

"Tommy Cavendish!" the bartender hollered out across the bar, forgetting to cover the phone's mouth-piece. "Sorry, doesn't look like he's here."

She tried Tommy's house. Neither he nor Claire was home. Then, on a hunch, she tried Alyssa Castor's number, the girl with the major crush on Tommy.

"Hello?" The voice was tentative and mouselike.

"Alyssa? It's Kat Ridgemont. I'm looking for Tommy. Tommy Cavendish?"

Silence.

"Have you seen him today?"

Still not a sound.

"Alyssa?"

"Why would you think I'd seen him?" came the frightened response finally.

"I thought you two were friends."

A small gasp. "Me and Tommy."

"If you should see Tommy, would you call me?" She gave the girl her cell phone number.

When Kat walked through the door of her house, she was almost surprised to find Emily at home, sitting in the living room, watching TV.

Emily picked up the remote and turned off the television as Kat came in. She looked guilty enough that Kat figured Angela or Angela's mother had told her that she'd been busted.

"Look, I know what you're going to say," Emily began.

"I don't think you do. Yes, I know you didn't spend the night at Angela's last night. But what has me upset is that you lied to me. Where were you last night? No more lies. You're going to be eighteen in a few months. By this time next week, you'll have graduated. Your life will be your own—with no interference from me."

"Hallelujah," Emily said under her breath.

"But until then, at least be honest with me."

"I was with Zachary Pierce," she blurted out, sounding close to tears. "I didn't want to tell you because I thought you'd make a big deal out of us dating."

Zachary Pierce? A boy from the most influential family in town? "You're dating Zachary?"

"Don't sound so surprised," Emily said. "I knew what you'd think. How could a Pierce ever be interested in a Ridgemont? You don't think I'm good enough for Zach, do you?''

"I didn't say that," Kat denied. "I just don't want him taking advantage of you."

"See, you think the only reason he'd date me is for sex," Emily snapped. "Well, you're wrong about him. He isn't like that and neither am I."

"Emily, you lied to me and spent the night with this boy—"

"We didn't do anything but talk!" Emily cried. "Zach likes me, Kat. He likes *me*."

Kat realized what she was saying. She went to her sister. "Of course he likes you. Who wouldn't?"

Em shrugged and smiled shyly. "You think?"

"I know." Kat hugged her, wishing she wasn't always suspicious—especially of men.

"I was with Zach," Em said, "the night someone broke into Dr. Manning's lab and vandals painted the side of Mr. McDougal's bait shop."

Kat couldn't hide her relief. "When I saw that red jacket—"

"I guess I left it at the arcade, but I didn't want to tell you that either. Not after I begged you to buy it for me. I knew you'd kill me if you thought I'd lost it."

"Don't worry about the jacket," Kat said. "It will turn up."

"It already has," Emily said, and looked up at her, a look Kat recognized too easily.

"Angela."

Emily nodded. "Her mother found out about the vandalism and grounded her."

"And the boys who were with her?" Kat asked, already knowing the answer.

"Razz and Dodie."

"They took the cadaver from Dr. Manning's lab?" It still surprised her they would do something like that.

"I guess it was just supposed to be a dare, breaking in, taking something," Emily said. "It was Angela's idea to take the cadaver. They were going to leave it on the school steps as a joke, but someone stole it."

"Is that the story they're telling?" Kat said.

"No, it's true. I guess they were offered a reward to return it and were going to take it back, but when they went to retrieve the body, it was gone."

Kat felt a chill. If they hadn't put the cadaver in the gazebo, then who had? The same person who'd left crushed daisies on her doorstep this morning as a warning? Had the cadaver also been a warning?

UNDER A MOON, swollen gold, and just a day away from full, Jonah drove out to Dr. Manning's, not sure what kind of reception he was going to get. Manning had had enough time to get rid of any evidence that might have been found in the lab. Any sign that the FBI agent before him might have gotten into the lab.

Nor did Jonah expect he'd find out what was coming into the country by boat.

Maybe Dr. Manning had nothing to hide. Or maybe Manning wanted his blood so badly that he'd slip up and show him something. Or tell him something he wouldn't mean to.

The gate opened before his motorcycle reached it, and closed swiftly behind him, making him a little uneasy. He couldn't help but remember what had happened to Kat after her visit here. What did Manning have planned for Jonah? After spending the entire day doing grunt work for Brody, Jonah was in no mood for games.

"Mr. Ries," Manning said, greeting him from the front door.

Jonah climbed off his bike and walked toward the house. "Dr. Manning. This place is too much, really."

Manning seemed to find some satisfaction in the fact that everyone thought his house was haunted. Jonah wondered if Manning knew about the vampire and mad scientist rumors—and helped perpetuate them.

Jonah only got a glimpse of the interior of the house—at odds with the outside, that was for sure—before Manning led him around to the back where the laboratory stood like a prison complex behind an electric fence. It appeared that a triple strand of razor wire had recently been added—no doubt after someone had stolen the cadaver found on the town green.

"You haven't changed your mind about being part of my research, have you?" Manning asked as he unlocked the complicated system going into the lab. Fort Knox should have such a system.

"Sorry, Doc, but I have a fear of nooses," Jonah joked.

Manning glanced toward the moon, then at Jonah. His look said he knew exactly what Jonah had to fear.

The inside of the lab was just as Manning had said it would be: boring. The doctor talked about his research. Jonah asked questions, getting the stock answers he had expected. Nor did he see anything suspicious, but then he didn't really know what he was looking for. It would take another scientist to recognize something amiss.

Other than getting the lay of the land, Jonah just hoped to leave a listening device. The last agent had been successful in leaving a bug in the house—but not the lab. It appeared Manning didn't do regular checks for listening devices—considering how long the one in the house had been in place.

Manning led him into yet another stark white, sterile room, walked to a table and pulled off a drape partially covering what looked like cages.

Jonah let out a gasp before he could catch himself.

"I told you I wouldn't disappoint you," Manning said with a satisfied smirk.

In the cages along the wall were hurdreds of rats and mice, but nearer, in a large cage, was a creature so shriveled and aged that Jonah didn't recognize it at first. "This chimpanzee has lived longer than any chimp in the history of the world, thanks to my research," Manning said, walking over to inspect the ancient primate. "Do you realize what it could mean to discover the fountain of youth?"

"Overpopulation," Jonah quipped. He could hear some animals in the next room banging around in cages. Wasn't that the fear of every Ries in his family, to end up in some laboratory cage being poked and probed and analyzed to death?

Suddenly, he just wanted out of here. But as he turned, he saw something in the adjacent room that horrified him, stopping him dead. A stack of small, child-size coffins lined one wall from floor to ceiling.

"Not all the chimps and monkeys enjoyed such long lives," Manning said, coming up behind him.

Jonah had seen enough. He'd managed to grab hold of the stainless-steel counter and plant the bug. He was ready to get out of there.

But Manning wasn't through with him yet. He opened another door and went to a massive computer console, pulling up an extra chair before sitting down. He motioned to the chair, but Jonah chose to stand. "I have something I want you to see."

With a couple of clicks at the keys, Manning brought up Jonah's family tree, then glanced over at him. "I don't think you realize how rare lines like yours are," Manning said fervently. "Your great-great-great-grandmother lived to be almost one hundred and ten. That was unheard of in her day. Your genes could change the world."

Jonah moved away from the computer and Manning. "I don't want to change the world."

"Don't you? Isn't that really why you went into the FBI? Aren't you an idealist, Mr. Ries? A man who thinks he can single-handedly make a difference? Imagine the difference I could make with just a small amount of your DNA?"

"You're barking up the wrong tree, Doc," Jonah said. "Even if I was the man you thought I was, there is nothing I'd like more than to see the Ries genes die off. And if I have anything to do with it, they will."

Manning looked thunderstruck. "You wouldn't continue the line?"

"The line is flawed, Doc. My parents are proof of that." He looked at his watch. It was after eleven and he was anxious to get to Kat. "Unless you have some jars with heads in them, I really need to get going."

Manning looked more than disappointed. He looked desperate. He clicked off the computer and got up slowly from the chair. "I had hoped you were a progressive thinker."

"I just want to get through this life as best I can," Jonah said truthfully.

Manning stared at him for a moment, a wild, disturbed look in his already scarier-than-hell gaze. Jonah realized he might have made a fatal mistake coming here.

But after a moment, the scientist walked him out to the fence that surrounded the lab, unlocked the gate and let him out. "If you change your mind…"

Jonah nodded, but it was clear from Manning's dour expression that he knew Jonah wasn't going to. But Jonah wondered if that would stop the doctor.

As he drove his bike back into town, he saw a woman cross Main Street and disappear into the cemetery. A feeling of déjà vu hit him. He slowed the motorcycle. The last thing he wanted to do was go into the cemetery, especially with the moon rising and almost full.

But he turned in, driving slowly, looking for Claire Cavendish. He got off his bike and wandered among the graves on foot.

He found her not far from McFarland Leary's grave, her body rigid with fear and trembling like the leaves in the oak overhead in the breeze.

"Claire," he said quietly.

She spun around, her eyes wide with terror.

"I'm Jonah Ries—"

"I know who you are," she said, her voice breaking. "I heard about you."

He didn't want to know what she'd heard. "Come on. You aren't ready for this, trust me."

She glanced back toward where Leary lay, then at Jonah. She nodded and let him lead her out of the cemetery, through a gap in the fence beside a huge old oak, the closest exit he knew of to her house. He offered her a ride home, but she turned it down, taking off the moment they hit the street. He thought about following her, but changed his mind. He'd followed enough young women home lately.

He started back toward where he'd left his bike and immediately heard the footfalls behind him. Two sets of soft-soled shoes. He waited for their attack, afraid he'd scare them off if he counterattacked too soon. He wanted to know who they were. But more important, he wanted to know who had sent them after him.

He didn't have to wait long. They came at him from behind, the heavier one charging him, the footfalls more pronounced than the smaller ones.

They bungled the attack badly, even if he hadn't been trained for just such an occasion. He had them both on the ground without even breaking a sweat.

"What do you want?" he demanded, his knee in the larger one's back, his hand around the other one's neck as he held them both down.

"Nothing," the littler one cried.

He recognized them as two punks he'd seen hanging around the arcade. "You don't jump someone for nothing," he said, putting pressure on both.

The larger one—Jonah thought his name was Razz—let out a squeal. "It was only a joke, man. We were just kidding around."

"Bull," Jonah snapped.

"No, really. We were just supposed to scare you," the other one—Dodie or something like that—said.

"Shut up, Dumbster," Razz mumbled.

"Who hired you to scare me?" Jonah demanded, pressing his knee into Razz's back.

"I don't know, man, really. We got a note saying to do it and we'd get some cash. I swear."

"It's true," Dodie cried.

Jonah applied a little more pressure, but the two stuck to their story, adding one small detail. They'd been paid to knock him out and take some of his blood.

He swore, imagining these two trying to take blood. They were to be contacted later to make the deal for the specimen. They swore they didn't know who was doing the buying.

He finally let them up, figuring Manning had to be behind the plan, although it seemed pretty amateurish for the doctor. The two scrambled off like hyenas.

When he reached Kat's, no one was home, the house locked up and silent. Anxious and worried, he tried her office on his cell phone. No answer. Damn. Where could she be? Maybe she'd gone to his apartment looking for him. His instincts told him she was in danger, but then he already knew that.

At his apartment, Jonah saw at once that someone had been there. When he opened the door, though, he didn't find Kat inside. Brody was waiting for him.

"Come on, you wanted in on this. I assume you have a gun?"

Jonah nodded, wondering what he had gotten in on, disappointed Kat wasn't here and all the more worried. "Where are we going?" He needed to find Kat.

"To meet a boat," Brody said, watching him closely. "The *Audrey Lynn.*"

Jonah pulled his .38 and shoulder holster from under the towels on the shelf, fighting two conflicting battles inside him: the need to find Kat and assure himself that she was all right. And the need to find out what was aboard the *Audrey Lynn* and solve this case before the full moon. His instincts told him that the cargo onboard that boat was connected to whomever was after Kat. But Brody offering him the chance to board the boat seemed almost too good to be true.

"Am I really going to need this?" he asked Brody as he checked the .38 to make sure it was fully loaded. It was.

"You never know," Brody said.

He didn't like the way his cousin said it. This wasn't like Brody to cut him in on anything. Every instinct in him told him he was walking into a trap.

Chapter Fourteen

At the wharf, Jonah followed Brody along the docks to a slip with a new thirty-five-foot fishing boat, complete with cuddy belowdecks and two two-hundred-and-seventy-five-horse motors on the back. The name on the side read *Wharf Rat II*.

"Nice," Jonah said, stopping to eye the boat.

"Come on, we have to hurry," Brody said, seeming nervous. But then, he always seemed nervous, now that Jonah thought about it.

"Maybe you'd better tell me what's on this boat we're supposed to meet," Jonah said.

Brody turned to look back at him, squinting under the dull glow of the wharf lights. "You don't know?"

He realized his mistake. If he was on the up-and-up, he wouldn't be asking around about the *Audrey Lynn* unless he knew exactly what was on that boat.

"Hey, you got me carrying," he said, patting his .38. "You're acting nervous as hell and you're wondering why I'm questioning what to expect when we get out there?"

"Don't worry about it, I'm just a little jumpy because we're running late since you were off doing who knows what," Brody said. "Now untie the damn boat and let's quit discussing this on the dock, all right?"

Jonah went to untie the bow. That was close. He knew his mind was on Kat. But if he hoped to get through this night, he'd better start paying attention to his job.

He boarded the boat and Brody started up the motors. Once out of the no-wake zone, Brody opened them up. It was a hell of a nice boat and it moved. There was something reassuring about that as the craft roared out past Lighthouse Island on the endless flat sea. The moon rode with them, a reminder that by this time tomorrow night, it would be full. Tonight, it painted the Atlantic pale silver, and had he not been a Ries, he might have thought it beautiful.

"Take the wheel for a moment," Brody ordered.

Jonah reached for the wheel. But the moment he touched it, Brody hit him in the arm. His body jerked, the pain like a giant bee sting. He'd looked down to see the syringe sticking out of his shirt, the needle buried in his flesh. Before he could reach for it, he'd dropped to the floor.

"I told you to stay away from Kat Ridgemont," he heard Brody say from some distance away, and yet he could feel Brody's large pudgy fingers pulling at his arms, dragging him across the deck. Then he was falling. For an instant, he thought Brody had dumped him over the side of the boat into the ocean. In his condition, Jonah knew he'd drown. His limbs felt paralyzed, his mind dazed.

But instead, he fell down a short flight of stairs. The last thing he remembered was Brody saying, "You're damn lucky my orders weren't to throw you over-board.'' Then a door slammed shut, the clear click of a lock snapping into place, followed by total darkness.

JONAH DIDN'T KNOW how long he'd been out. He woke in a small cramped space, nauseous, head aching and hurting, caught up in a dream in which he kept hearing Kat calling to him. The spot on his arm hurt like hell where Brody had injected him with who knew what. It ached down to the bone. Whatever drug Brody had given him had left him weak and queasy.

By sheer determination alone, he managed to strug-gle to his feet, making as little noise as possible. He could feel the boat still moving fast. Did that mean they hadn't reached the *Audrey Lynn* yet? Or were they al-ready on the way back?

He felt for his weapon. Gone. No big surprise there. He tried pushing against what felt like the door with his body, then smacking it hard with his shoulder. But the space was too small to get enough leverage, and Brody must have moved something in front of the door because it didn't even budge. So Jonah waited, won-dering what was planned for him, knowing whatever it was, it wouldn't be Brody's call.

He must have dozed off again from the drug. When he woke, the boat was slowing down. He could hear the whine of the outboards. He listened, wondering where they were.

Then the engines died. The boat wallowed in its own wake for a few minutes. He couldn't hear any music from the bars along the wharf. Nor the sound of any other boats. As far as Jonah could tell, they were still out at sea.

The boat banged into something solid. A dock? Or another boat? Then he heard Brody's voice calling out to someone.

Jonah only caught some of the conversation. It appeared Brody might be haggling over something, probably price. He heard a thunk overhead as if someone had jumped aboard. Then the boat pitched and yawed as something was being loaded aboard. "Be careful with those!" he heard Brody call out.

From what Jonah could tell, the crew loaded five boxes, wooden, from the sound of it, and heavy enough to make scraping noises when set down.

He tried the door again, putting more shoulder into it, hoping the sound on the deck would cover his attempts to break out of his confinement.

"Shh. Give me a minute," he heard from the other side of the door. His heart caught in his throat as he recognized Kat's voice. "Thank God you're finally awake. I was worried that he'd killed you."

He heard a scraping sound against the door as something heavy was being pushed aside. The door opened, the sudden light blinding him.

Before he could ask Kat what the hell she was doing here, gunfire filled the air over their heads. Three shots, followed by another three in quick succession.

He grabbed for Kat, pulling her down as he scanned the lower deck, looking for something to use as a weapon. His gaze settled on her. "You don't happen to have that little Beretta…?"

She pulled it out of her purse and handed it to him.

"I don't know what the hell you're doing here but I am damn glad to see you."

"The feeling is mutual."

"Stay here. Hidden. Don't come out unless I tell you to." He listened for a moment, hearing nothing, and then he moved cautiously up the steps toward the deck. The moon shone down like a spotlight. He could hear the water lapping at the side of the boat and feel the fishing boat bumping against what he figured was the larger boat, the *Audrey Lynn.*

As he peered out into the moonlight, he could see the larger vessel, a rope ladder hanging down. Brody's body lay sprawled on the deck in a pool of blood. He winced, not surprised at the way his cousin's life had ended, but still sorry to see it.

Just past Brody were five boxes, the size big-screen televisions came in, only these were made of wood. It was too dark to see what had been printed on the sides.

He waited for a few minutes before he bounded up the steps to crouch behind the boxes. He'd expected to hear gunfire, expected someone to take a potshot at him.

But all he could hear was the water and the boats as they thumped restlessly together where Brody had tied them up.

Still being cautious, he edged toward the rope ladder, knowing he would have to climb up into the larger vessel to see if all the merchandise had been unloaded onto the fishing boat. Also if anyone was still alive aboard the *Audrey Lynn.*

He waited, the Beretta feeling small and insignificant in his hand, then he moved quickly. First to Brody's body, where he scooped up Brody's weapon, and then up the ladder. He figured Brody hadn't fired an entire clip. At least he hoped not.

But when he bounded onto the deck of the *Audrey Lynn,* he realized he wasn't going to need any fire-power. Three bodies lay in moonlit pools of blood. He checked, all dead. It didn't take but a moment to realize the skeleton crew had stayed onboard to deliver this shipment while the others must have gone ashore.

Hurriedly, Jonah checked to make sure all the boxes had been unloaded before the shootout. He could find no others that resembled the ones on the deck of the *Wharf Rat II.*

So what had Brody done? Shot everyone after the boxes were loaded as a double-cross? Was this the last shipment he ever planned to get? Otherwise, it seemed like a dumb move, burning his bridges like that.

Jonah looked around to make sure there was no one else onboard the *Audrey Lynn,* then, climbing back down to the *Wharf Rat II* again, he untied, moved to the wheelhouse and started up the outboards, quickly pulling away from the larger vessel.

"Kat," he called as soon as he was a safe distance from the *Audrey Lynn.*

She scrambled topside and into his arms. "Oh, God," she breathed against his neck as she spotted Brody. "Is he—?"

"Yeah. Want to tell me what you're doing on this boat?"

"I came to your apartment to tell you something I'd discovered, and found a note on your door from Tommy Cavendish to meet you at the *Wharf Rat II* on the docks. I'd just found out earlier that Tommy bought the only bottle of perfume like the one my mother used to wear from the drugstore in town. Someone had special ordered it, but never picked it up, no doubt knowing they would put it on the shelf. I wanted to warn you about Tommy, so I stowed away on the boat.''

He looked at her, fearing she thought that made perfect sense. ''You could have gotten yourself killed.''

''That was what I was trying to avoid,'' she snapped.

He held her to him, breathing in the scent of her as the boat sped north, just glad to have her in his arms, to have her safe. They had less than twenty-four hours before the full moon. They had the cargo from the *Audrey Lynn*. But they also had Brody's dead body sprawled on the deck. They couldn't take the boat back to Moriah's Landing, that was for sure.

A few miles up the coast, far enough away from the *Audrey Lynn* to feel a little safe, Jonah stopped the boat, found a crowbar in Brody's tools and began to pry open one of the boxes on deck to see exactly what he was dealing with. What was it that had gotten the other agent killed?

Kat held the flashlight as the lid on the top box creaked open a crack. He pried harder. The lid gave. The beam of the flashlight filled the dark hole.

Kat gasped, dropping the light as she stumbled back. The smell alone almost knocked Jonah to his knees as he picked up the flashlight and shone it down into the box.

''What was that?'' he heard Kat ask breathlessly.

''A mummified body.''

''It's…hideous.''

Jonah couldn't have agreed more, the image of the wild hair, the sunken eye sockets, the grinning teeth… That on top of the drug Brody had given him earlier…He shone the light on what he'd seen printed to the side of each box and felt his stomach lurch.

Each box was marked with a woman's name, the name of the cemetery in England where her body had been stolen from and a pentagram—the sign of a witch.

"Why would anyone want those?" Kat said in a whisper a few feet away from him.

"For research," he said, more to himself than to her. These mummified bodies were worth a fortune to any scientist in the secret society. The question was, who'd brought them from England?

"What are we going to do with them?" she asked.

He started to reach for his cell phone. It was time to involve the FBI. But he never got it from his jacket pocket before he saw the figure appear from its hiding place on the far side of the boxes closest to Kat.

Jonah went for Brody's gun that he'd stuffed into his shoulder holster while he'd pried open the box. But he wasn't fast enough.

The figure grabbed Kat around the neck and dragged her to him, putting a gun to her head. "Don't think I won't kill her."

Chapter Fifteen

Jonah had forgotten about Deke. Obviously the forty-eight hours that the feds could hold him were up. But from Deke's expression and the weapon he had pointed at Kat's head, Deke hadn't forgotten.

"Thought you had me locked up, didn't you, you bastard," Deke said, pulling Kat tighter against him, the barrel of his gun at her temple. "I *knew* you were back in Moriah's Landing. The moment the feds hit me with some trumped-up interrogation crap, I knew."

"She doesn't have anything to do with this," Jonah said, not interested in the chip on Deke's shoulder. All he cared about was Kat. "Let her go."

Deke smiled. "Just goes to show what you don't know about anything. Speaking of knowing something, I know you're wearing that shoulder holster, the one you were always so fond of. Reach inside real easy, pull out that gun you took off poor Brody and kick it over here. Then we'll talk about me letting Kat here go."

Did Deke not realize that Jonah still had Kat's little Beretta? He'd stuck it in the waistband of his jeans, under his coat.

''Come on, we don't have all night,'' Deke snapped. There was a mean edge to his tone. Deke had been furious when Jonah had taken the stand, his testimony putting the former agent behind bars for three years. Deke should have gotten a lot more, but he made a deal and got off with a light sentence.

Obviously, even a short prison stay didn't seem to have done him any good. If anything, Deke seemed more angry and vengeful.

But what was the hurry? Why didn't they have all night?

Jonah pulled Brody's weapon from his holster, slowly, carefully, pretty sure Deke was just aching to kill him, and at the same time wondering what Brody had done with his .38. Probably thrown it overboard. Was there any chance he'd put it down belowdecks? Put it somewhere where Kat might have found it while Jonah had been on the *Audrey Lynn?*

He could see her face in the moonlight, her dark blue eyes questioning as if waiting for him to tell her what he wanted her to do. He hadn't noticed before, but she wore black jeans and a large black sweatshirt. He met her gaze, trying to send her a message from his mind to hers. *Everything is going to be all right. You don't happen to have the .38 by any chance?*

Unfortunately, he couldn't sense what she was thinking. She looked scared, but not terrified. He hoped she didn't try anything. Deke would kill her just for the fun of it. Just to see Jonah suffer.

No, he thought. Deke wasn't going to kill her. The thought came to him clear as day. That decision wasn't up to Deke. Someone else was running this show—a man who wanted Kat alive because the moon wouldn't be full until tomorrow night.

Deke was just a hired gun, his only qualification for the job: he hated Jonah Ries enough to kill him.

Jonah kicked the gun over to Deke and watched Kat grimace, her hand going to her right side as Deke pulled her down to pick up the gun. He threw it into the Atlantic, never taking the barrel of his weapon from her temple.

"Now let her go," Jonah said, trying to sound bored by all this. "Then we can talk about making a deal. Do you realize what's in those boxes?"

"Something that smells like hell."

"Something worth a small fortune, if you know who to offer them to," Jonah said.

Deke looked interested, greed pushing aside good sense as he shoved Kat over to the box Jonah had opened. "Damn, what's in there?" he asked, obviously having gotten another whiff of the contents.

"Mummified dead women," Jonah said, remembering that Deke had always been squeamish when it came to dead bodies, something to do with his grandmother and a spilled casket when he was little.

"Not just dead women, dead witches," Jonah added, knowing how superstitious he was, as well.

The one thing that didn't faze the ex-FBI agent was killing. It had to be impersonal enough, as long as he could just blow people away and split. But Deke had a thing about distancing himself from the dead. "You never want to look a dead person in the eyes," he'd once told Jonah. "They'll take you with them, sure as hell."

"How much money?" Deke asked, motioning to the boxes full of bodies. "These are for genetic experiments, aren't they? Hell, they must be worth a fortune. I mean, how many old dead witches are there to dig up?"

Deke wasn't as stupid as he looked.

"First, you let Kat go." Jonah had to know if this strong, sure feeling was on target.

Deke looked sincerely bummed. "I can't do that, I'm afraid. You see, she's part of the deal I made and it's a deal I can't go back on. I know what happened to the last agent."

"What did they do to Max?" Jonah asked, trying to keep the anger out of his voice.

"They fed him to the fish," Deke said flippantly. "The same thing they're going to do to you."

Jonah could hear a boat motor in the distance. Someone was coming. They must have had a tracking device on Brody's vessel and were now homing in on them. Soon Jonah wasn't going to like the odds.

He noticed Kat was still holding her right side, but the look in her eyes had changed. If only he could know what she was thinking. All those years of fighting his mystical heritage. He took a chance. One hell of a gamble.

"You kill her and they'll do a lot worse than that to you, won't they?" Jonah said. Slowly, he pulled the Beretta from his waistband. Deke yelled for him to stop. Jonah held his breath as he leveled the barrel at Deke's head, afraid he'd hear a gunshot, afraid he'd just cost Kat her life.

"Let her go, Deke. She isn't worth dying over. You

can tell them I got the jump on you. They'll believe that.''

Deke looked scared but not convinced Jonah would take the shot—not with Kat's head so close to his. ''Sorry, Jonah, but I think we got ourselves a Mexican standoff here. You pull the trigger, I kill your girlfriend. In a few minutes, it will all be moot anyway.'' The other boat was getting closer, the motor roaring as it bore down on them.

''Maybe not,'' Kat said as she lifted the sweatshirt to reveal Jonah's .38. In one swift movement, she pulled it and stuck the barrel into Deke's ribs. There wasn't much he could do, considering one hand was holding the pistol to her head and the other arm was wrapped around her neck.

He tightened his hold on her neck, but she slammed the .38 deeper into his ribs in reprisal.

Deke swore. ''You bitch!'' He shoved her, sending her flying across the deck at Jonah.

Jonah got off one shot. He saw Deke grab his left arm as he dived over the side of the boat. There was a splash, then nothing but the sound of the other boat, so close now Jonah could see only its bow as it barreled down on them.

The boat slammed into the side of theirs, knocking Jonah to the deck, the Beretta skittering across the fiberglass out of his reach as Brody's craft keeled over at a forty-five-degree angle.

The boxes with the mummified bodies tipped, the highest ones toppling over. One of them burst open as it hit the deck, bones scattering.

Kat had gotten to her feet just moments before.

She'd had her back turned to the oncoming boat, watching Jonah. He hadn't had time to warn her before the boat hit. She went down hard. He heard her head hit the deck and then she didn't move.

A spotlight shot down from the larger vessel that had hit them broadside, blinding him as he tried to grope his way to her.

''No!'' he heard someone cry out. ''Don't hurt her!'' Tommy. It was Tommy Cavendish's voice. Then the sound of feet hitting the deck as someone jumped aboard Brody's boat.

Jonah crawled over to Kat. The last thing he remembered was touching her cheek, realizing how cold it felt, then seeing the blood pooling beneath her head. Something hard struck his skull and the lights went out.

KAT WOKE TO THE SMELL of fish, the sound of water lapping at wood and darkness. She opened her eyes, instantly aware of the pain. Her fingers went to the back of her head. She winced at the knot the size of a goose egg just above her ear.

Someone had bandaged her head. For an instant, that gave her hope. Someone who planned to hurt you wouldn't dress your wounds, would they?

She tried to sit up, realizing she was on some sort of table or bench. In a boathouse? She could feel the gentle rocking. She was definitely on the water. But as she pulled up, she heard the jangle of chains, then pain shot up her right wrist as something cold cut into her flesh and jerked her back down.

Rolling onto her right side, she looked down. Her eyes had begun to adjust to the light. It wasn't total darkness. A little light leaked in through the cracks in the boards of her prison. But it still took a moment for what she saw to register.

Her right wrist had been handcuffed to a piece of pipe fastened to the wall next to the bench where she lay. She pulled to see if the pipe would give, hoping... It didn't. That's when she noticed her right leg was also chained to the pipe.

Panic raced like fire through her. Someone had left her here to die. She went rigid with fear. Her pulse thundered in her ears. She fought to catch her breath. She opened her mouth and tried to scream. Only a small, insignificant sound escaped. She tried again, her scream bouncing off the walls then dying away in echoes. She screamed again and again until her throat hurt, her head pounding.

No one came. She heard no other sound, except for the water lapping at the boards. She'd thought she might be near the abandoned cannery building by the wharf, but someone would have heard her. And her captives would have known that. They wouldn't have left her in a place where she could be rescued. Not that easily.

She lay back down, her head aching. She wasn't going anywhere. She had to stop panicking. She had to think. Her first clear thought was of Jonah. Where was he? Tears rushed to her eyes. She wiped them away hurriedly with her free hand. Crying wouldn't help. Nor hoping for Jonah to rescue her. She was on her own.

She waited until her heartbeat slowed enough that her head wasn't pounding, then she sat up and looked around the room she was in, searching for something to use to pry the pipe. While it appeared to be well fastened to the wall, the boards had to be weakened by the years and the saltwater. She hoped.

She spotted an old wrench on the floorboards not far away. But how could she reach it? She wasn't that far off the floor. In fact, she could drop her left hand a few inches over the side of the bench. But she was still about a foot short of touching the wrench. What did she have that she could use to lasso the tool? She looked down, assessing what she had on. Not the jeans. Or the sweatshirt. Nor would she be able to tear the material to make a rope.

Suddenly, her head didn't hurt quite so badly as she remembered that she'd worn a belt. Hurriedly she began to work it free from her jeans with her left hand. If she could make a loop at the end... If she could drag the wrench over close enough... She went to work, noticing as she did that the sun was sinking over the Atlantic, amazed she'd been out for so many hours. It wouldn't be that long before she was pitched into the blackness of night. Until the moon rose up over the ocean. And tonight, the moon would be full.

JONAH WOKE to the sound of Deke's voice and just assumed he'd died and gone to hell.

"Why are you keeping him alive?" Deke demanded some distance away. "You said I could kill him."

At first Jonah thought the sobbing he heard in the background was Kat. He forced his eyes open, his head aching from where someone had hit him. He didn't know how long he'd been out. His mouth felt dry as cotton and, as the floor beneath him pitched and rolled, he realized he was sick to his stomach. They must have drugged him again.

He closed his eyes, trying to ignore the way the floor moved. He must be on a boat. Nothing else moved quite like this. He thought he could hear the motor, felt the vibration as the boat moved through the water. It wasn't Kat crying.

He opened his eyes and lifted his head just a little. Deke was still arguing. Jonah could see him silhouetted against the light. Another figure sat just out of view. The sobbing came from the corner. Jonah looked that way, but instead of Kat, it was Tommy Cavendish, his head on his knees, his arms wrapped around his legs.

Jonah stared at him, willing the boy to look up. It took all his strength, but after a few moments, Tommy did look up. Even from here, Jonah could see the dried blood on the boy's mouth and shirt. He locked eyes with Tommy for a moment, then let his head fall back, closing his eyes to the sickness that washed over him.

"Get someone else to unload those boxes," Deke was saying. "Man, they stink. I'll puke if you make me do it."

"Then puke," snapped a voice. "But shut the hell up."

Jonah felt his heart drop in his chest, his stomach roiled as he recognized the voice. Maybe he was dead. Maybe they were all dead. Definitely in hell.

"I think Jonah's awake," he heard Deke say. "I think I saw him move."

Someone prodded at him with a pole. He tried not to react, but did. Slowly, he opened his eyes, afraid of what he'd see. A man stepped into view, a face peering down at him.

"Tell me we're all dead and in hell," Jonah said, his voice only a whisper, his mouth was so dry.

Missing FBI agent Max Weathers smiled down at him. "I'm the only one who's dead and I plan to stay that way."

"Let me kill him now," Deke demanded, pushing his way into Jonah's vision. "The bastard shot me." Deke held up his bandaged arm.

"It was just a flesh wound," Max said impatiently. "We're almost there. I need you to unload the boxes, then you can kill him."

"To hell with that," Deke snapped. "You unload your own damn boxes. I told you, they stink, and whether you like it or not, I'm wounded and it's a lot more than a damn flesh—"

The gunshot resounded through the boat, so close Jonah could smell the powder, almost feel the recoil. Deke grabbed a handful of Jonah's shirt as he went down, pulling Jonah up from the boards. Deke hit the floor, blood gushing from the chest wound as his grip on Jonah's shirt suddenly released.

"Now you're wounded," Max said as he returned his weapon to the holster at his back.

Overhead, someone yelled down that they had the dock in sight. Jonah felt Max look down at him. He shifted his own gaze from Deke's dead body to the agent standing over him, hoping Max would tell him he was still working undercover and not to worry, he had everything under control.

But the moment Jonah looked into the man's eyes, he knew that wasn't going to be the case.

"I can either pump you more full of drugs or tie you up, your choice," Max said. "I'm being paid to deliver you alive or I'd just as soon shoot you."

That was clear enough. "No more drugs," Jonah managed to say, pretending he was more out of it than he was.

"Okay," Max said, grabbing up a length of nylon rope, making Jonah wonder who had been tied up before him. Kat? "Where is she?" he managed to say.

Max studied him as he bound his hands. "You'll see her again."

Jonah couldn't help the hope that surged through him. "Then she's alive?"

Max nodded as he bound Jonah's ankles together with a separate piece of rope. As he finished, he glanced toward the porthole. "For the time being, she is."

Jonah closed his eyes and willed his body to go to sleep—at least to appear that way. He could hear Max still standing over him listening as his breathing dropped into a steady rhythm, his eyelids fluttered, his pulse dropped. Max didn't seem to remember Tommy huddled in the corner crying as he left. No doubt he thought he had the boy completely cowered. Jonah feared he did.

The moment Jonah heard Max's tread on the stairs, he opened his eyes and looked over at Tommy. The boy had his head down again, but raised it as if sensing Jonah looking at him. Jonah tilted his chin, motioning the boy over.

"Untie me," Jonah whispered. "Hurry."

For a moment Tommy stared down at him, his face frozen in fear. "He'll hurt me again," the boy whispered.

"He'll kill Kat if you don't help me," Jonah whispered back with a knowing that it was the only thing that could get the boy to help him.

Tommy hesitated only a moment, then began to work at the knots at Jonah's wrists.

KAT HOOKED THE END of the wrench with her belt and began the slow, torturous drag across the weathered boards toward her. It was awkward with her left hand. She'd already hooked the tool numerous times, only to have the belt slip off. Her arm ached and she felt sick with worry that her attempts were futile. She was running out of time.

The sun had sunk in the sky off to the west. She could see the darkness through the cracks in the wallboards. Soon the moon would rise, round and golden, and she knew whoever had left her here would come back for her.

Slowly, she pulled the wrench closer. Now all she had to do was get the loop to slide up the heavy tool. Just a few inches, just so she could get some leverage. If she did it quickly enough, she could grab the wrench before it slid all the way through the loop and dropped to the floor again.

But she'd had it at this point so many times and hadn't been able to move quickly enough. It meant letting go of the belt and grabbing the tool in just that instant.

Her head ached and she knew the queasiness in her stomach was making it harder for her to maneuver the wrench. As if using her left hand wasn't awkward enough.

She held her breath as she lifted her arm slowly. The tool rose, higher and higher. Any moment it would begin to slide. Just a little higher. She let go of the belt and grabbed for the wrench, her fingers brushed the cold steel.

For a moment, she thought she'd missed again. She waited to hear the clatter of the tool on the boards below her. Then she looked down at her hand and saw that her fingers had closed around the end of the wrench. She'd done it!

Now if she could just use it to pry the long piece of pipe from the wall. She could slide the other end of the cuffs off and she would be free.

She wedged the wrench between the long pipe and the wood of the wall and pulled with all her strength. She felt it give! She almost let out a whoop. She pried again. The screws that held the long pipe in place pulled out of the weathered wood at one end.

She hurriedly went to work on the other end, excitement making her giddy. She refused to let herself think beyond getting the handcuff free of the pipe.

The other screws gave. She jerked the long pipe to her, then worked the metal loop of the handcuffs down it until she was no longer attached to it. She sat up, rubbing her wrist, then her ankle.

The sun was long gone. Darkness had filled the room. In the distance, she heard a sound. Hurriedly she slid off the bench and worked her way to the door she'd seen earlier, the handcuff attached to her ankle dragging on the floor. She'd half expected the door to be locked. But then why handcuff her if that was the case?

The door swung open, the hinges groaning. She looked out to see nothing but ocean—and a small narrow walkway. She stepped out. The walkway appeared to circle the building she'd been in. She started around it.

Even before she turned the second corner, she knew what she'd find. It was a floating dock, moored far out to sea. On it was the small building she'd been held prisoner in. As far as the eye could see there was nothing but water. Her only option would be to swim, only she had no idea which way to go or how far from land she might be.

She felt tears well in her eyes, blurring the flat surface of the sea as the moon rose up from the water, a round ball of fire, turning everything it touched to gold. She heard him behind her and wondered how long he'd been waiting on the far side of the building.

She turned, just wanting it to be over. She couldn't take any more disappointments. Wherever Jonah was, he couldn't help her now and she had no way to help herself.

He came toward her, backlit by the full moon. It wasn't until he was almost to her that she saw he had one hand behind his back, the other outstretched. As he grew closer, she saw what he held out to her. A bouquet of white daisies tied in a worn red ribbon.

Chapter Sixteen

Kat looked from the daisies up into his face, her heart a hammer in her chest.

"You look so much like your mother," Ernie McDougal said shyly. "I loved her, you know. She said she didn't love me." He shook his head. "She said a lot of things, but I knew she did love me. Why else would she always tease me at the diner." He smiled at the memory, his eyes turning glassy in the moonlight.

She could find no breath to breathe, let alone speak as she stared at him, remembering his shyness and his moment of confusion at the bait shop. A thought hit her between the eyes: *He'd had the kids spray paint his building just to get me to come over.*

"Mr. McDougal, you're making a mistake," she said, the words coming on short, hard breaths. "I'm not my mother."

His smile faded. "Why did you tease me like that if you didn't love me?" He sounded pathetic, certainly not someone her mother would have ever looked at twice. Except at the diner, where she teased and taunted and raked in the tips. Ernie had never stood a chance with her mother. What had made him think he had?

"I bought you such pretty things. Like this white scarf." He brought his other hand out from behind his back and held up a white scarf.

It was all Kat could do not to scream at the sight of it.

"I know you liked that. You wore it all the time. You said you liked the way it moved in the breeze. Pure silk. You'd never had a silk scarf before. I heard you tell Marley as much." He smiled, caught up in the memory.

Kat thought she heard something over the sound of his voice and the lap of the water at the boards beneath them. A boat. She could hear a boat motor in the distance.

Ernie's gaze seemed to settle on her again. "You do like the scarf, don't you?"

"Yes." It took all the strength she could muster to reach out and take the scarf from his hand. She could see that he was waiting for her to put it on.

She remembered what he'd said about her mother liking it because it blew in the breeze. Would whoever was on the boat see the white scarf? Would they come over to investigate?

With trembling fingers, she tied the scarf around her neck.

Ernie smiled. "I know you like the perfume, too. No one bought you anything so expensive, you said. You wore it all the time. I heard you tell Brody that a real man bought it for you. You wouldn't have said that if you hadn't meant it. I saw the look in your eyes when you said it.''

She listened for the boat, the sound growing closer. She felt the scarf flutter in the breeze. Did she dare try to wave to the boat? What would Ernie do?

''You put the daisies in a vase and you would look at them and get that dreamy look in your eyes,'' he said, his voice quavering. ''You called me your secret admirer.''

His words finally registered. Oh my God. It was just as Jonah had suspected. Unrequited love. Ernie had never told her mother that he was the one who'd left her the gifts. When she wore the scarf and the perfume and bragged about the flowers, he'd overheard her in the diner. He'd thought she felt something for him, and all the time she'd had no idea it was Ernie McDougal.

His gaze hardened as he looked at Kat. ''You said such vicious things to me tonight in the gazebo. I just wanted to walk you home. It was so hard for me to finally tell you that I loved you. But I thought with the full moon...'' He shook his head. ''You shouldn't have said those terrible things to me.''

She saw him tighten his hold on the daisies, crushing the stems in his fist, the veins in his suntanned arms bunching.

''You're right, I shouldn't have,'' she said quickly, reaching out for the daisies, her hand shaking.

He looked up in surprise, his eyes shiny with hope in the moonlight.

''You just surprised me,'' she said, imagining how her mother had reacted at the news that her secret admirer was just Ernie.

The boat motor slowed. Ernie didn't seem to notice. She could hear it headed this way. Someone must have seen the white scarf in the moonlight. If only they would come close enough…

THE MOMENT TOMMY freed Jonah's hands, he tore at the rope binding his ankles. "I want you to hide. Go back deep into the boat and hide. Don't come out unless I tell you to, do you understand?"

Tommy nodded. "You're going to help Kat?" he said in a hoarse whisper. "I didn't know they would hurt Kat."

Jonah nodded and got up, glancing toward the stairs to the upper deck. Then he knelt over Deke's dead body, realizing he was starting to make a habit of taking weapons off dead men. He pulled out the .44 magnum, checked to make sure it was fully loaded, not surprised to find it was.

He looked back to see that Tommy had gone to hide, then he headed for the steps, wondering how many men were topside. As he started up the stairs, the boat began to slow. He listened, hearing nothing but the throb of the motor, then the boat banged against a dock and he heard Kat's scream for help.

He bounded up the stairs. Max didn't hear him coming. Only when he came flying out from belowdecks did Max turn and try to go for his gun, but Jonah never gave him a chance to fire. He pulled the trigger on the .44 magnum, hitting the rogue agent in the chest twice before Max's body could drop to the deck.

Then Jonah swung the barrel around as a crew member dived for him. The bullets caught the man in the throat and shoulder. Jonah stepped back as the man crumpled at his feet. Another one of the crew tried to make a run for it, diving overboard. Jonah let him go, swinging around, following the direction he'd heard the scream come from.

He saw the scarf first. It billowed out in the breeze, stark white in the moonlight. She stood on what appeared to be a floating dock, looking as if she was waiting for a boat.

For a moment, Jonah didn't see the man in the shadow of the boathouse. Then Ernie McDougal stepped out to encircle Kat's waist. The blade of the knife in his other hand glittered in the moonlight as he drew it slowly across her neck, just above the scarf, the tip touching just enough that it drew blood.

Kat cried out, but held perfectly still.

Jonah froze, the gun in his hand wavering as he stared in horror at the scene before him.

"She doesn't love you, Ries," Ernie said, his voice flat. "She loves me."

Jonah saw the terror in Kat's face. And the hope. She needed a superhero, a man with powers that Jonah Ries did not possess. And yet the night out at Dr. Manning's, he'd stopped her car. Had it only been out of sheer will? Or was the answer in the genes he'd so despised all of his life?

He looked at Ernie McDougal, concentrating on the hand holding the knife, knowing what Ernie planned to do, sensing it like nothing he'd ever felt before. Ernie was going to kill her. As he'd killed her mother. Only this time, he planned to take his own life. There was nothing Jonah could do to stop him. Nothing short of willing him to move the knife away from Kat's throat, knowing that one slip and it would be over.

Silently, he sent it like a prayer, all his senses on the hand holding the knife. All his will on saving Kat. He cursed the years he'd denied who he was, what he was, and gave in, opening his soul to those who had gone before him, pleading for their help now.

KAT TOLD HERSELF she would never know exactly what happened. The doctors said her ramblings were from her loss of blood. Hallucinations. Why else would she have thought she'd seen the ghosts of women floating over Jonah, their spirits glowing in the moonlight.

All she knew was that one moment Ernie had a knife to her throat, the cut he'd made burning, his arm around her crushing the breath from her. Then she'd felt his body begin to tremble, the hand with the knife jerking away from her throat.

She'd acted out of instinct, she supposed, since she couldn't remember thinking before she buried her elbow in Ernie's stomach. He stumbled back, teetering for a moment on the edge of the dock. She could still see him suspended there, trying to regain his balance, the knife in his hand, his eyes on the blade as if it had a life of its own.

And then, with no warning, Ernie had plunged the knife into his own heart. He'd looked up then, his gaze connecting with hers, then he'd fallen backward into the ocean.

She'd expected his body to surface again, but it didn't. Then Jonah was there, taking her in his arms, frantically trying to stop the bleeding from the cut on her neck, a cut she could no longer feel. All she knew was that she was in the safety of his arms and nothing else mattered.

Later in the hospital she would remember the pounding of the boat, the wind blowing the tops off the waves, showering then both with cold salty water as Jonah rushed her toward Moriah's Landing.

The storm had come out of nowhere, waves crashing over the deck of the boat, washing away the boxes and the bodies inside. Through the spray, she had seen Lighthouse Island, the lamp burning brightly, and she'd thought of her father. How many times had he rushed toward the light, trying to get home?

Once, she had looked back into the moonlight darkness thinking she could still see the dock, almost thinking she saw Ernie in the water, pulling himself up. But she knew that had only been her fear making her imagine it. Ernie wouldn't be coming back and she didn't even question how she knew that.

It wasn't until they'd reached the hospital that someone, maybe Jonah, had untied the white scarf around her neck. It had been white, hadn't it? Funny, but she now remembered it as being bright red. Red as blood.

"You are not going to die," she'd heard Jonah say as she was rushed down the hall on a gurney. He'd held her hand, squeezing it, but his voice had sounded far away. "You are *not* going to die. If it takes everything in me, I will not let you die."

She remembered smiling up at him and saying something about superheroes and powers and tarot cards and true love.

But when she'd closed her eyes to rest, she realized that none of it made any sense at all.

She might have seen her mother. Her father had been waiting for her in a room filled with light, but he sent her back, saying she wasn't finished yet. After that, she slept.

JONAH LEANED OVER THE bed to plant a kiss on Kat's forehead. She slept, the sleep of angels, her face peaceful.

"How is she?" Cassandra asked from the doorway.

He nodded her in.

His cousin joined him. She wasn't wearing her caftan nor her bracelets. She wore jeans and a blouse, her hair dark like his again. "I'll buy you a cup of coffee," she offered. "The doctor said she'll sleep for another two hours and twenty-seven minutes."

He smiled at that, knowing no doctor had said that. Kat would be awake just before dawn, in exactly two hours and twenty-seven minutes. That didn't leave him much time. He looked down at her, his heart bursting and said "I love you" in his mind, hoping she would hear it.

"You saved her life," Cassandra said when he joined her in a corner of the empty cafeteria. Outside, darkness hunkered in the trees, the moon full and glowing.

Had he saved her life? He couldn't be sure. So many things had happened: Ernie, the storm, all that blood. He could still see Kat's pale face and feel the life seeping out of her as he raced toward Moriah's Landing, willing her to live with all the strength in him.

"I've decided to stay in Moriah's Landing. Ernie was going to put the Bait & Tackle shop up for sale. I'm gonna buy it. I'll be needing a partner if I want to make it a true charter business," Cassandra was saying. "Ernie was too busy fronting for the secret society to make much out of it."

Jonah nodded. It had all come out, Tommy being the real hero as he told the cops how Ernie had smuggled in the bodies of witches from around the world for a member of the secret society's genetic research. Unfortunately, the latest shipment of bodies had been washed overboard and lost at sea. Nor was it known who the intended buyer was. Ernie had taken that to his watery grave.

"Unless you're thinking about staying with the FBI?" Cassandra said.

He hadn't thought about it until that moment, but he knew he'd changed since he'd come back to Moriah's Landing and could never go back to the way he was. Just as he couldn't go back to the FBI.

"Maybe Kat would like a partner," Cassandra said, and smiled.

Yes, he thought, he had a feeling Kat would like that.

"I take it you're no longer…involved with Dr. Manning?" Jonah asked, curious why she'd helped the man cheat at poker.

"It got me in the game, which was amusing for a while." Cassandra smiled. "And profitable. I hadn't planned to stay any longer than the summer. But then you showed up."

It would take some getting used to, being around

Cassandra, someone who knew him almost better than he knew himself. It would take even more getting used to having a family again.

"When are you going to tell her?" Cassandra asked, glancing back down the hall toward Kat's room.

Suddenly he saw it. The white house near the sea, the swing set in the backyard, the three kids and Kat, the sunlight pouring down on them, the sound of laughter as they turned to look back at him.

Cassandra swung her gaze back around to him. She smiled. "Unless, of course, you've changed your mind about having a family of your own?"

He finished his coffee. "Thanks."

Cassandra shrugged. "What did *I* do?"

As if she didn't know. "I suppose I don't need to tell you where I'm going?"

Her expression turned somber. She shook her head and reached out to grasp his hand. She squeezed it. "Good luck."

They both knew where he was headed would take a lot more than luck.

MIST ROSE from St. John's Cemetery and moved restlessly through the gravestones. The old wrought-iron gate groaned as Jonah pushed it open and stepped onto the hallowed ground. He could feel a vibration deep inside him as he worked his way through the moonlit stones.

He felt them all, the peaceful sleeping the sleep of eternity, the restless turning in their coffins, all reaching out to him as he made his way to the graves of his parents.

He hadn't been here since both had been laid to rest. Now he stood over the matching headstones, the moonlight at his back. Betrayal comes in all forms. Betraying your heritage was the worst in a family like his.

But he'd come home now. And he planned to stay. That meant admitting who he was. What he was. It wouldn't be easy. His parents knew that better than most. They had taken their lives rather than know so much about the world and the lost souls in it.

He bowed his head, reaching out to them as he hadn't in life, finally feeling that elusive sense of peace he'd so yearned for as he accepted the legacy that had been handed down for too many generations to count.

As he raised his head, he looked through the maze of tombstones to McFarland Leary's grave. Hadn't he always known this is where it would end? Slowly, he worked his way through the mist rising around him, the moon full and high as if watching him. It was time to face the true ghost of his past.

KAT OPENED HER EYES as the sun came up over the sea. The first face she saw was Jonah's. He smiled as he took her hand and touched his lips to the palm, opening her fingers, opening her heart.

"I love you," he said, his gaze meeting hers.

She couldn't help but smile, as much as her neck hurt where Ernie had cut her, one nick almost lethally too deep. "I love you." The words came so naturally. Her heart felt like a bubble inside her, blossoming with that love.

"There's something I have to tell—"

She touched her fingers to his lips, afraid he was going to tell her they couldn't be together.

He kissed her fingertips and then captured her hand in his. "I don't know what happened last night, I just know that I love you, I can't bear the thought of living a day without you, but last night changed things."

She held her breath.

"If you're crazy enough to marry me—"

"More than crazy."

"—you have to know you'll be getting all the family…quirks that come with me. And," he said before she could interrupt, "so will our kids."

Kids? She felt her heart soar, remembering what Cassandra had told her. Tears welled in her eyes and spilled over.

"Our children can have two heads and I will still love them just the way I love you," she said.

"I don't think you're taking this seriously."

She smiled as she looked into his amazing face, knowing in her heart she wouldn't be here now if it wasn't for this man. "I'm taking it very seriously. And counting on our children getting at least some of my down-to-earth plain old common senses. Even if they don't, I'll be around to try to keep you all grounded. So are you going to do this the right way or not?"

He smiled at her, shaking his head as he dropped to one knee beside the bed. "Kat Ridgemont, will you marry me, keeping in mind the kind of man you'll be marrying?"

She laughed. "I know exactly what kind of man I'll be marrying," she said, throwing her arms around his neck. "Yes!"

Behind him, she caught a glimmer of light, and for a moment she thought she saw images hovering in the shadows smiling down on them as he took her in his arms.

She closed her eyes, not sure what she believed anymore. Except, if there really were gifts that could be passed from one generation to the next, she planned for hers to be the gift of love.

*   *   *   *   *

And the story continues....
Next month don't miss
the next installment of
MORIAH'S LANDING:
SCARLET VOWS
By Dani Sinclair

Prologue

Eerie stillness blanketed the morning air over Moriah's Landing. The troubled town brooded beneath the sweltering heat, expectantly waiting.

Her customers all served for the moment, Brianna Dudley pushed at the damp tendril of hair clinging to her forehead and wiped her hands on her apron. Even in the air-conditioned diner it was too hot. A sense of something about to happen crawled over her skin.

A scan of the horizon through the diner window failed to reveal any gathering clouds. She'd hoped that might account for the unease whispering over her nerve endings. Storms always made her tense.

Brie inhaled the chilled air in the diner uneasily. Yvette Castor raised a summoning hand from her solitary seat in a booth near the window. Her many-ringed fingers waggled, the multitude of bracelets clanging merrily as she motioned for her check.

"Anything else, Yvette? More coffee?"

"No thanks. I have to get over to my shop. Cassandra is off today and I'm doing an early-morning reading for one of my regulars."

Yvette had become a part of the local color in more

ways than one. Today's bold purple peasant blouse clashed cheerfully with most of the colors in her skirt.

Running Madam Fleury's fortune-telling stand across the street from the diner suited Yvette. At times there was an almost mystical quality about the woman. Brie couldn't imagine her doing anything else.

"How is your mother today, Brianna?"

The reminder of her mother's drawn features this morning made Brie grimace. "The heat's getting to her."

More than the heat, and both women knew it. There was no way Brie could pretend any longer that the cancerous tumor hadn't returned. After the last attempt to remove it, Dr. Thornton warned if the tumor began to grow again, it would only be a matter of time.

Brie swallowed hard against the knot at the back of her throat. Her hand quivered as she handed Yvette her check. Their fingers collided. A warm tingle spread like waves of invisible energy right up Brie's arm from that point of contact. For a timeless second, everything seemed to stop. Yvette seemed to gaze straight inside her soul.

Brie yanked her hand back. Yvette grasped the check before it could flutter to the tabletop. Her gaze never wavered.

"Do not worry," Yvette said quietly. "Closure is at hand."

A stab of genuine fear made Brie inhale sharply.

"No! I'm sorry, Brianna. I phrased my words poorly. I didn't mean your mother." She offered an apologetic smile. "I should have said, 'Your prince is coming.'"

"Now, what on earth would I want with a prince?" she joked, though she was clearly rattled. "I already have enough people to serve." Brie indicated the diner at large, beginning to fill with the usual morning crowd. "And I'd better get back to work before I get fired."

"Brianna."

A warning prickle scaled its way down her spine. Unable to leave, but not wanting to hear any more talk about princes, or discuss her mother's illness, Brie tried to force her legs to take the necessary steps away from the table. She couldn't.

"Things happen for a reason, you know," Yvette said softly. "You must learn to trust your heart once more."

For a moment, his features were right there in her mind, as vivid and alive as the man himself. Brie could almost see the way the sun placed golden highlights in his hair. She could almost smell the scent of the ridiculously expensive aftershave he wore. And without even closing her eyes, she felt the power of his body as he drew her into the embrace she had craved for what seemed like eternity.

"No!"

Brie lowered her voice quickly. No one spared her a glance. She tried for a smile, but was only partially successful. "Forget it, Yvette. I made the mistake of trusting my heart once before. It didn't work out."

Yvette gazed right through her pretense. "Was it really a mistake?"

Jolted, Brie mustered a glare. Everyone knew Brie's young daughter, Nicole, was the joy of her life. While definitely an unplanned pregnancy, her daughter's birth was a gift.

"So maybe it wasn't a total mistake," she conceded. But her foolish, stupid heart gave its usual lurch at the memories she had never learned to suppress. "But falling in love is a mistake I won't ever make again."

"Perhaps that was not a mistake either, just mistimed."

Brie suppressed a bitter laugh. "Oh it was mistimed all right. Take it from me, Yvette, I learned one important fact the summer Nicole was conceived. Princes have a disturbing habit of turning into frogs."

She tore her gaze from the sympathy and understanding in Yvette's sad expression, acutely grateful for the gruff, burly biker who indicated he and his companion were ready to place their order.

"I'll be right with you, Rider," she called out. To Yvette she added lightly, "Thanks just the same, but I'll pass on any more princes. I don't have time for fairy tales anymore."

Or the Pierce family—Andrew Pierce in particular. Nicole's father.

"Fairy tales can come true," Yvette said softly.

"Ha! Mine would need a fairy godmother with the cure for cancer. If you meet any, feel free to send them my way. Have a good day, Yvette."

Brie moved briskly to where the two scruffy-looking bikers waited with stoic patience.

Andrew Pierce was undoubtedly some woman's idea of a prince, she thought, but not hers. Not anymore.

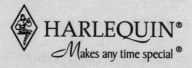

TRUEBLOOD, TEXAS

Coming in April 2002...

SURPRISE PACKAGE

by

Bestselling Harlequin Intrigue® author

Joanna Wayne

Lost:

Any chance Kyle Blackstone had of a relationship with his gorgeous neighbor Ashley Garrett. He kept flirting, but she wasn't buying.

Found:

One baby girl. Right outside Kyle's apartment, with a note claiming he's the father! Had Kyle just found a surefire plan to involve Ashley in his life?

Ashley was determined to stay away from the devilish playboy, but the baby was irresistible...then again, so was Kyle!

Finders Keepers: bringing families together

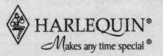

This Mother's Day Give Your Mom A Royal Treat

Win a fabulous one-week vacation in Puerto Rico for you and your mother at the luxurious Inter-Continental San Juan Resort & Casino. The prize includes round trip airfare for two, breakfast daily and a mother and daughter day of beauty at the beachfront hotel's spa.

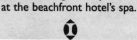

INTER·CONTINENTAL
San Juan
RESORT & CASINO

Here's all you have to do:

Tell us in 100 words or less how your mother helped with the romance in your life. It may be a story about your engagement, wedding or those boyfriends when you were a teenager or any other romantic advice from your mother. The entry will be judged based on its originality, emotionally compelling nature and sincerity. See official rules on following page.

Send your entry to:
Mother's Day Contest

In Canada
P.O. Box 637
Fort Erie, Ontario
L2A 5X3

In U.S.A.
P.O. Box 9076
3010 Walden Ave.
Buffalo, NY
14269-9076

Or enter online at www.eHarlequin.com

PRROY

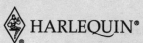
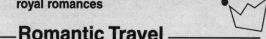

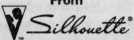

April 2002 brings four dark and captivating paranormal romances in which the promise of passion, mystery and suspense await...

Experience the dark side of love with

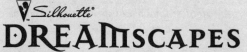

DREAMSCAPES

WATCHING FOR WILLA
by *USA Today* bestselling author Helen R. Myers

DARK MOON
by Lindsay Longford

THIS TIME FOREVER
by Meg Chittenden

WAITING FOR THE WOLF MOON
by Evelyn Vaughn

Coming to a store near you in April 2002.

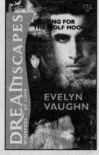

Where love comes alive™